Questions bombarded him.

Questions about the bank robbery and questions about his attraction to a woman with a baby.

He'd sworn off putting his heart on the line. He'd had his shot at a family and happily-ever-after and it had been snatched from him when his wife had died in childbirth.

So why couldn't he get the pretty mother out of his mind?

Tossing aside the covers, he padded to the window that overlooked the lake. Peering across, he could see Maggie's house lit up like a Christmas tree.

Realization hit him.

She was all alone and scared. And with the threat the robber had left ringing in the air, she would be jumping at every creak and moan of the house.

Without a second's hesitation, he picked up his phone and dialed her cell phone. She might be afraid of the phone ringing at this time of night, but his number and name were programmed in her phone. Once she saw it was him, she would be all right.

Books by Lynette Eason

Love Inspired Suspense

Lethal Deception
River of Secrets
Holiday Illusion
A Silent Terror
A Silent Fury
A Silent Pursuit
Protective Custody
Missing
Threat of Exposure
*Agent Undercover
*Holiday Hideout
The Black Sheep's Redemption
*Danger on the Mountain

*Rose Mountain Refuge

LYNETTE EASON

makes her home in South Carolina with her husband and two children. Lynette has taught in many areas of education over the past ten years and is very happy to make the transition from teaching school to teaching at writers' conferences. She is a member of RWA (Romance Writers of America), FHL (Faith, Hope, & Love) and ACFW (American Christian Fiction Writers). She is often found online, and loves to talk writing with anyone who will listen. You can find her at www.facebook.com/lynetteeasonauthor or www.lynetteeason.com.

Danger *on the* Mountain

LYNETTE EASON

Love Inspired

Recycling programs
for this product may
not exist in your area.

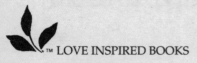

™ LOVE INSPIRED BOOKS

ISBN-13: 978-0-373-44510-3

DANGER ON THE MOUNTAIN

Copyright © 2012 by Lynette Eason

www.LoveInspiredBooks.com

Printed in U.S.A.

You are my hiding place; you will protect me from trouble and surround me with songs of deliverance.
—*Psalms* 32:7

To my Lord and Savior who lets me do what I do.
I love you, Jesus!

ONE

Deputy Reese Kirkpatrick stiffened when he felt something hard jam into his lower back. He started to turn when a voice whispered in his ear, "Get on the floor or the baby's mama gets a bullet."

Stiffening, his adrenaline in sudden overdrive, Reese looked around and saw a young woman with a baby in a carrier standing in front of the teller's window. As his adrenaline spiked, details came into focus. The teller's nameplate said Lori Anglero. The woman with the baby had soft blond hair that fell to her shoulders in pretty waves. The man behind him had bad breath and needed a shower.

Reese's time as a cop on the streets of Washington, D.C., now served him well. He didn't even blink. "You think this is going to work for you?"

"Yep. You're the only man in here. I don't need you having a hero complex because I'm trying to do this without killing anyone. But I will if I have to. On the floor. Now."

The door chimed one more time, and Reese caught sight of two more masked men entering the First National Bank of Rose Mountain.

"Everybody down! Now!" The man behind Reese gave him a hard shove.

Reese dropped, grateful he wasn't wearing his uniform

and that the gun hidden under his coat in the small of his back had gone undiscovered.

Screams echoed and Reese saw the woman in front of Lori's window drop down to become a human shield for the baby.

"Down! Down!" The man who'd taken Reese by surprise aimed his gun and pulled the trigger.

The bullet slammed into the wall above Maggie Bennett's head. With a scream, she tightened her protective stance over her eight-month-old daughter's carrier.

Terror spiraling through her, Maggie whipped her head to the left to see three gunmen in black masks. One stood by the door, his broad shoulders and tight grip on the pistol in his left hand saying he'd be a force to reckon with. Another, tall and lanky, hovered in a threatening stance over the man on the floor. The third held his weapon in a way that said he knew how to use it—and would. The tall, skinny one with his weapon trained on the man on the floor grunted, "Charlie, get the cash."

Charlie leaped over the counter. As he did, his foot caught the nearest silver pole holding the red velvet ropes used to separate customers into lines. The pole crashed to the tile floor with a loud clang, and Maggie cringed. Charlie cursed, regained his footing and pointed the gun in bank teller's terrified face. "You deaf? I said get down!"

The teller dropped.

So did Ashley O'Neal, the other teller who'd been so friendly to Maggie last Sunday at church.

At three o'clock on a Monday afternoon, Maggie and the man now on the floor were the only customers in the bank. She watched his hand angling under his heavy suede jacket.

What was he doing?

Her eyes darted from robber to robber, to the door then back to the man on the floor.

There was no security guard and no help in sight.

The broad-shouldered one who stood by the door appeared to be in charge. He jutted his chin toward the man on the floor. "Cover him, Slim. He looks like he might be thinking he wants to put up a fight."

Still hunched over Belle's carrier, Maggie felt strangled by her fear and she wasn't sure what to do. She was frozen in place, watching the incidents playing out before her as though they were on a big screen and she was in the audience.

But she wasn't. This was real. And it was happening to her.

Her first reaction was to look for a way to protect Isabella. Her second to silently screech out a desperate prayer as she slumped to the floor next to the fallen pole, keeping herself between the men and her baby. Her foot became entangled in the rope now snaking the floor, but she ignored it. Her only thought was to keep her cool and survive. Old instincts surfaced, and a chill that matched the November air outside the bank swept through her.

As her eyes jumped from one robber to the next, she let her gaze land on the other bank customer. He lay still, left hand away from his side, right still hidden by his jacket. His sharp green eyes took in the unfolding scene. Maggie could see the tension in his shoulders and face and prayed he didn't do something stupid, like try to be a hero.

He'd get them all killed.

"You!" Charlie yelled at the teller who'd been helping Maggie. "Stand up!"

The woman obeyed, tears tracking her cheeks, hands raised as she backed up away from her station. "D-don't shoot me. Take what you want."

Slim continued to hold his gun on the man on the floor while Charlie threw a large bag at Maggie's teller. "Load it up. Now."

The woman caught it, fumbled it, shot a terrified glance at the man, then went to work. Even from her spot at the last teller station next to the wall, Maggie could see the woman's hands shaking.

"Hurry up!" The lookout man next to the door shifted, the chink in his calm demeanor grabbing Maggie's attention. So he wasn't as cool about this as he'd first appeared.

Charlie shot him an aggravated look, his eyes piercing and hard behind his mask. "Just watch the street."

Then he turned back to jab the teller with his weapon. "Move! Move! This ain't a tea party!"

Lori's hands shook so hard Maggie was afraid she'd drop the cash and the man would shoot her. She almost offered to help but bit her tongue. As long as Lori was getting the money in the bag, Maggie would stay quiet and keep her body covering Belle's. She darted a glance in the direction of the offices. One door was closed. The bank manager in hiding?

She prayed that no one else would walk in and this would all be over in a few seconds. Dark spots danced before her eyes, and she realized that she was holding her breath. She gasped in air. The dancing spots disappeared, but Belle started to cry. Maggie froze.

The lookout lifted his gun and pointed it at her. "Shut the kid up."

Immediately, Maggie knelt and unbuckled Belle from her car seat. Picking her up, she settled the baby against her and turned her back to everything going on. Belle sniffed and lay her head on Maggie's shoulder, thankfully content to be out of the carrier and to suck on the pacifier Maggie shoved in her mouth.

Maggie glanced over her shoulder as Charlie hauled himself back on the other side of the counter and held up the bag. "Got it!" His gaze landed on Maggie and she stilled, not liking the look in his eyes.

Slim spoke. "Get the other drawer."

"We don't have time for that, Slim," the lookout protested. So maybe Slim was the one in charge?

Charlie ignored his partner and slung the bag back at the teller who moved to the next drawer.

Sirens sounded and the three masked men exchanged a glance. Slim growled, "Who tripped the alarm? Who?"

The robber nearest the door immediately turned and disappeared through it.

Maggie saw the well-built customer on the floor clench his jaw even as he slowly moved his hand back under his jacket.

The door burst back open. "The cops are almost here! I got the car! Let's get this done!"

Slim looked up and his gaze slammed into Maggie's. "Get over here."

She froze once again, arms gripping Isabella too tight. The baby hollered her displeasure, and Maggie shushed her even as her eyes met the narrowed brown ones of the man who'd ordered her to move.

"My name's Reese Kirkpatrick. I'm a cop. You've got what you want, you'd better leave while you can."

Maggie jerked her gaze to the man on the floor. He'd been silent throughout the whole ordeal. Silent and watchful. Slim raised his gun and brought it crashing down toward Reese's head. Reese rolled. Slim missed and stumbled, his finger jerking the trigger. The weapon bucked in his hand, the bullet shattered the tile floor beside Reese's left leg.

Reese now had a weapon pulled and aimed at Slim. Without a word, he pulled the trigger.

Slim screamed and jerked as his gun tumbled to the floor.

Charlie whirled and dropped the bag of money as he moved toward his wounded partner. He lifted his weapon, aiming toward Reese who was now moving across the floor toward Slim. Charlie's left leg stepped in the midst of the red velvet ropes.

Without thinking of the possible consequences, Maggie jerked on the rope.

Charlie went down hard, the back of his head cracking against the floor. Reese lunged for Slim and snagged the mask. It came off and Slim howled his outrage even as he landed a lucky blow with his good hand to Reese's solar plexis.

Reese grunted and stumbled back, gagging. Slim looked like he might go after Reese again, but the screaming sirens outside seemed to change his mind and with a final glance at the unconscious Charlie, and a hard glare at Reese, he backed toward the door, hand held tight against the wound in his shoulder. "I'll kill you for this!" His gaze landed on Maggie and she flinched when he said, "Her and the kid, too!"

Reese finally got his feet under him, snatched the weapon from the unconscious man on the floor, then stumbled after the wounded robber. But by the time he hit the door, the man was in the car. The door slammed shut halfway down the block.

Reese whirled back into the bank and checked to make sure Charlie was still out cold.

He was.

Next he checked on the woman with the baby. She sat

on the floor, eyes dry, jiggling her infant in her lap. He noticed the ringless left hand. And wondered why he would notice such a thing at a time like this.

"Are you all right?"

She lifted soul-deep dark brown eyes to his and the fear in them felt like a sucker punch to his midsection. Her low "Yes" vibrated through him. Then she drew in a deep breath and a tinge of color returned to her pale cheeks. "Yes, we're all right. Thank you." Then the baby turned her attention to him, spit out the pacifier, stuck a finger in her mouth and grinned around it.

This time it was a blow to his kidneys.

He nodded and turned, hoping his desperate need to get away from them didn't show on his face. He forced his mind to the matter at hand. Thank goodness she'd kept her cool over the last few minutes. If she'd been the hysterical type, they might all be dead. His ringing ears testified to just how close the gun had been to his head when it went off. He just hoped the ringing wasn't permanent.

"Is it over?" One of the bank tellers—the one named Lori—peered over the edge of the counter, mascara streaking her cheeks.

Grateful for the interruption—and the fact that he heard her, Reese nodded. "All except for the cleanup."

More tears leaked from her eyes and he saw her lips move in a grateful, whispered prayer.

Rose Mountain Police cruisers pulled in. Eli Brody, sheriff of Rose Mountain, bolted from the first one like he'd been shot from a cannon. The man strode toward him and Reese quickly filled him in. Eli snapped orders into his radio and two cruisers immediately headed out after the escaping getaway car. He then marched toward the other two officers, leaving Reese to question the tellers.

"Thank you."

The quiet words captured his attention and he turned to see the woman with the baby gazing up at him. Clearing his throat, Reese said, "You're welcome."

"I'm Maggie Bennett." She shifted and before Reese could gracefully slip away, she blurted out, "Was he serious? Do you think he'll come back and—" She bit off the last part of the sentence, but the fear lingered and he knew exactly what she was asking.

Reese shook his head. "I don't think you have anything to worry about. All those guys care about is getting away."

Doubt narrowed her eyes. "But we made him really mad. And you have one of his partners in custody because I interfered. We saw his face. You honestly don't think they'll be a tad upset about that?"

So she had spunk and she wasn't comforted because he told her what she wanted to hear. She wanted the truth, no matter what. He liked that.

He said, "All good points. The fact is, I don't know. We'll take precautions, get his picture from the bank camera and distribute it around the town. But as for whether he would really come back here…" He shrugged. "I'm sorry, I can't tell you."

"No, you can't." A sigh slipped out and she placed a kiss on the baby's forehead.

A baby girl with big brown eyes like her mama.

A knife through his heart wouldn't be any more painful. He had to get away. He'd come to Rose Mountain to escape memories of a wife and baby who were no more. Grief was sharp. Growing up in foster families, all he'd ever dreamed of was having a family of his own. And he'd had that for a while. Until they'd died.

"What's your baby's name?" He couldn't help asking.

"Isabella. But I call her Belle."

She said the name with such love that his heart spasmed once again. "That's a pretty name."

Her face softened as she looked at the baby in her arms. "Thanks. It was my mother's."

Was. Past tense. Her mother was dead. He recognized the pain in her eyes. The same pain he saw when he thought about his own mother who'd died when he was nine. Clearing his throat, he asked, "Do you need to call someone? A husband or…?"

"No, no one." A different sort of pain flashed in her eyes for a brief moment and Reese wondered what that story was. Then he blinked and told himself it wasn't his business.

A bank robbery was.

She was saying, "You said you were a cop. I don't remember seeing you around here before."

"It's my first week." He shook his head. "I just moved here from Washington, D.C. One of Eli's deputies quit, he needed another one and asked me if I'd take the job." He lifted his shoulders in a slight shrug. "Eli caught me at the right time. I was ready for a change." Eli said he'd seen something in Reese that had been familiar, something Eli had experienced only a few years before. Burnout.

A weariness of the soul. And grief.

And why was he sharing this with her? There was something about the way she looked at him. As though she really cared about what he had to say.

"Maggie, are you all right?"

Reese snapped his head around, and Maggie's gaze followed his to see Eli bearing down on them. The man's thunderous expression said the bank robbers had escaped.

Maggie nodded. She'd met Eli her first day in town. His wife, Holly, owned the Candy Caper shop on Main Street and when Maggie had stopped in for a bite to eat, Eli had been having lunch with Holly. They'd asked her what she was doing in town, and she'd told them she was looking for her grandfather's old cabin. They'd helped her move in, and they'd been friends ever since.

"I'm fine," she said. "Shaken, but fine."

"I see you've met Reese."

"Yes." She tried to smile. "He saved the day, I do believe."

Eli lifted a brow. "Oh?"

Reese shifted, the flush on his face revealing that he wasn't comfortable with the praise. "Just doing my job."

"Not even on the clock yet and already a hero, huh?"

"All right, that's enough," Reese said, his mild tone not hiding his embarrassment. "Maggie's the one who kept me from getting shot."

At Eli's raised brow, Maggie shook her head and refused to let Reese turn the attention back on her. However, she let him off the hook as she shifted Belle to her other hip. She couldn't help shivering as she remembered the look in the one robber's eyes. "He was going to make me go with him," she whispered.

"What?" Eli demanded.

She nodded. "If Reese hadn't intervened, the robber would have taken me and Belle with him."

Eli snapped a look at Reese. "That true?"

"It sure looked that way."

Eli's frown deepened. "Robbing a bank is serious business, but they were willing to add kidnapping, hostage taking, to it?"

"They were." Reese's nose flared. "And not only that, but one of them threatened Maggie and her baby—and me—as he escaped."

Now Eli's brow lifted and he reached up a hand to stroke his jaw. "Do you feel threatened?"

Reese looked at Maggie. "I'm not worried for myself, but I think you should make sure you have extra patrols around Maggie's place."

So he was worried about her.

Eli nodded. "I can do that, but she's pretty isolated out there on the lake."

"The lake?" Reese asked. "Which one?"

"Rose Petal Lake. Not too far from your place, I don't think."

Maggie spoke up. "I'm staying in my grandfather's old house. I'm trying to decide if I want to stay there permanently or get something here in town."

"Maggie teaches school," Eli said.

"Which one?" Reese asked.

"It's an online academy," Maggie said as Belle leaned over, trying to wriggle free of the arms that held her. Maggie expertly kept the baby from tumbling backward and said, "I teach fifth grade. It allows me to earn a living and keep Belle with me." And allowed her to try to figure out if she'd ever return home. She stiffened her spine. No, that house had never been home.

For the past six months, Rose Mountain had been home. And she didn't see that changing in the near future.

Eli scratched the back of his head, and Maggie felt Reese's gaze on her and Belle. And it unnerved her that every time his eyes landed on Belle, he looked away. In fact, other than asking her name, he hadn't acknowledged her presence. Did he not like babies? Children? Disappointment shot through her.

Squelching the unexpected feeling, she hugged Belle closer and said, "I've got to get her home for a nap. She's going to start getting cranky if I don't."

Eli nodded, placed the strap attached to his camera around his neck and said, "I just finished a weeklong crime scene processing training class last month." His lips quirked. "Thought I should update my skills just in case, but the whole time I kept wondering why I was there." He looked around and shook his head. "Guess now I know."

Maggie had lived in Rose Mountain long enough to realize that small town law enforcement officials often had to take care of the forensics side of things. If the nature of the crime warranted a higher level of expertise than the local sheriff, he had to call someone from a bigger city. Eli said, "You'll need to see the psychologist about the shooting and file a report."

Reese grimaced. "I know."

Eli nodded. "Why don't you see the ladies home, and I'll finish up here."

"Uh...yeah, sure."

He looked caught, trapped with no way out. She frowned. What was his problem?

Then he smiled and she wondered if she'd imagined the whole expression. She settled Belle back into her car seat carrier and he led her to the door. Stepping outside, she breathed in the fresh fall air, grateful to be alive.

"Which one is your car?" he asked.

"The blue Ford pickup." He looked surprised, and she laughed. "Didn't expect me drive a truck, did you?"

"No, I was looking for a minivan or something."

Maggie clucked her tongue. "Shame on you. Stereotyping?"

He grinned, and she felt that tug of attraction she'd been hoping she wouldn't feel again. The last thing she or Belle needed—or wanted—was a man in their lives. His eyes held hers a bit longer than necessary. She looked away as he said, "Yes, I guess so. Sorry."

Maggie settled Belle into the back of the king cab and opened the driver's-side door. Climbing in, she noticed Reese watching. He gave her a nod and let her lead the way. Pulling out of the bank, she turned right onto Main Street. As she drove, she listened to Belle chattering in the backseat. At least she hadn't suffered as a result of their scary adventure this morning.

Soon, she'd have to feed the baby her afternoon bottle or her sweet chatter would turn to demanding howls.

Maggie headed up the mountain, the short mile to her home seemed to take forever. Pulling into the gravel drive, she cut the engine and waited for Reese to drive up beside her.

He climbed out and looked around. He pointed. "See that house just across the lake?"

"The one with the white wraparound porch?"

"Yeah. That one's mine."

"It's beautiful. I noticed it the day I moved in." Maggie pulled the carrier with the sleeping Belle from the backseat with a grunt. She slid the handle onto her arm up to the crook of her elbow. "She gets heavier every day, it seems like."

He shut the door for her and asked, "Where's Belle's father?"

"Dead." She heard the matter-of-fact tone in her voice.

When she turned, surprise glistened in his eyes. "I'm sorry," he said.

"I am, too. Sorry he's dead, not sorry he's out of my life."

TWO

The woman just kept surprising him. The gentle, mommy demeanor hid a spine of steel. Also evidenced by her cool-under-fire reaction at the bank earlier.

Opening the door, she led the way inside, holding the carrier in front of her. "I'm surprised she's still sleeping." She set the baby carrier on the kitchen table and opened the refrigerator to pull out a bottle filled with milk.

"Why aren't you sorry he's out of your life?"

While Maggie placed the bottle in a pot of water she began heating on the stove, she kept her back to him. He wanted to turn her around so he could see her face. When she didn't answer, he leaned against the counter and crossed his arms, wondering why he was asking questions that were none of his business.

At first he thought she was going to pretend she hadn't heard him, but when she turned, she said, "I shouldn't have said that."

Reese lifted a brow at her.

She shrugged and grimaced. "He wasn't a very nice person."

He'd abused her. She didn't say so, but she didn't have to.

His gut tightened as visions of women he'd pulled out of domestic violence situations crowded his mind. Their bruises, their damaged faces, bodies…souls. The ones who had died. He blinked the images away and focused on Maggie.

"When did he die?"

"About a month after Belle was born."

"Car accident?"

Maggie sighed. "Not exactly."

She didn't want to tell him?

Belle woke suddenly and let out a howl. Reese flinched and watched Maggie calmly unbuckle her daughter from the car seat and pick her up. She then pulled the bottle from the heated water, tested the temperature of the milk on her wrist and stuck it in the squalling mouth.

The silence was sudden.

"You're good at that."

Maggie laughed. "I've had a lot of practice."

As the baby ate, Reese took in his surroundings. "Nice place."

She looked up from Belle's face to smile at him. "I like it. It's simple, functional and pretty much everything Belle and I need."

He nodded. "You said you were an online teacher."

"I am. I teach learning disabled students online. It's perfect for us. I get to make a living and Belle gets to stay home with me. So far so good."

"What about when you have to teach and Belle doesn't want to cooperate with your schedule?"

Maggie grinned. "I have a neighbor who comes over. Mrs. Adler. She's a retired nurse and lives twelve hours away from her grandchildren. She loves Belle and acts as if every moment she gets to spend with her is the high-light of her day."

A shadow moved across the window right in his line of

sight. He straightened and narrowed his eyes. She caught his expression and frowned. "What is it?"

"Probably nothing," he said. "Just thought I saw something move outside of your window." He walked over to it and, out of habit, stood to the side, keeping himself from being a target should someone other than a friend be out there. The blinds were open, the sun high in the sky.

What had he seen?

Anything at all?

Or was he still jumpy from this morning? He saw Maggie settle into the rocking recliner next to the couch, Belle's small hands clasped firmly on the bottle she eagerly devoured. In his mind's eye, he replaced the scene with one containing Keira and his own baby girl. But that wasn't to be. Sorrow clamped hard on his heart, and he had to make a supreme effort to shut the feeling down.

He was in Rose Mountain, making a new start. There was no place for sorrow or sad memories. Two things he'd been desperate to get away from back in Washington. "I'm going to check outside around your property."

Her frown deepened. "You think someone is really out there?"

"I don't know, but it won't hurt to check."

Worry creased her forehead as her eyes followed him out the door.

Once outside, he stood still, taking in the sights and sounds he'd become familiar with in such a short time. Nothing seemed out of place. Nothing set off his internal alarm bells.

He made his way over to the window in the den. The open floor plan had allowed him to be standing in the kitchen, looking into the den. If he'd kept his eyes on Maggie and her daughter, he'd never have seen the shadow.

If that's what he'd seen.

Circling the perimeter of Maggie's house, he kept an eye on the area around him and on the ground in front of him.

With Thanksgiving just around the corner, the air had a bite to it. He shivered, wishing he'd grabbed his coat on the way out. The hard, cold ground held no trace of any footprints. No evidence at all that anyone had been in front of the window.

Then what had caught his attention? Anything? Or was he so on edge that he was now seeing things?

He frowned, shook his head and walked back into the house to find Maggie still holding Belle. The baby swiveled her gaze to him and he swallowed hard when she grinned. Two little white front teeth sparkled at him.

Maggie asked, "Did you find anything?"

"No. It was probably just nerves left over from this morning."

She shot him a doubting look. Fear flickered in her eyes before she turned back to Belle, who'd finished her bottle. Maggie settled the baby into a sitting position and started a rhythmic patting on the small back. Her actions were automatic, but her eyes said her thoughts were on their conversation. She asked, "You think it could be the man who said he'd kill us?"

Did he? "I think that guy's long gone."

Maggie bit her lip and he wondered if she believed him. And he couldn't blame her. He wasn't sure he believed it himself. She sighed. "So what's next?"

"We'll question the robber in custody, see if he'll talk for a deal."

Maggie shuddered. "Did you see his face? His eyes? They were hard. Empty. I don't think he'll be talking any time soon."

"Don't be so sure." He glanced again at Belle who stood on Maggie's thighs, holding on to her mama's hands. Reese averted his gaze. "I'm going to head back to the station and see if he's said anything."

"All right." Maggie stood and shifted Belle to her hip. "She's got a nap to take, and I've got an afternoon class to teach." She paused. "Will you keep me updated on what happens? I'm still a little nervous about that threat."

He smiled, hoping to reassure her. "Sure thing."

Maggie walked him to the door and locked it behind him. Then she walked into Belle's room and placed the sleepy baby in the crib. Even though Belle had fallen asleep for a short time on the ride home from the bank, she needed a real nap or by the evening, she'd be so cranky Maggie wouldn't know what to do with her.

Belle protested for a while, but she finally fell quiet, her cries fading as she slipped into sleep.

Maggie smiled. It had been so hard to learn to let the baby cry, but once she'd tamped down her instinct to hold Belle every time it was naptime, they were both a lot happier. Belle slept better, and Maggie was able to get a few things done.

Like teach her online class. She still had about ten minutes before she had to sign in. Mrs. Adler should be arriving soon. The woman lived just a few houses up from Maggie and often walked over to be there in case Belle woke up while Maggie was in the middle of a class. Maggie paid her a weekly wage, and Mrs. Adler was thrilled to be making money and honing her grandmother skills.

With Reese's dominating presence gone, she now felt an absence she'd never noticed in the small house before. What shocked her was her lack of nervousness when he was around. She'd actually let him in the house. The fact that he was a cop helped. She felt safe with him in a way she didn't feel with other men who were not in law enforcement. Officers had helped her when she needed it most. Like Felicia Moss, the officer who'd listened to Maggie's story and then taught her how to hide once she escaped from Kent.

All that knowledge, and she hadn't needed it. Kent had been killed before she could put into practice everything she'd learned.

Gulping, she pushed aside the memories and booted up the computer. Signing in, she greeted the students already in the room and got started.

Forty-five minutes later, she signed off, thanked God once again for the ability to work from home and got up to check on Belle. Sleeping soundly.

Mrs. Adler had slipped in and was sitting in the recliner reading a book. "Hello there."

The woman set the book in her lap and looked up to smile at Maggie. "Hi. Belle's sleeping away, and I'm enjoying a good book. How'd your class go?"

"Great. I only had three show up today, and we had a fascinating discussion about right angles."

Mrs. Adler grimaced. "Please don't talk about math. I still get hives if I have to think about numbers without a calculator in front of me."

Maggie laughed. "I love math. I actually prefer it." A noise outside the door made her jump and turn. "Did you hear that?"

"Hear what?"

Shivers danced in her stomach, but she didn't want to alarm Mrs. Adler unnecessarily. "Um…I thought I heard Belle. Do you mind checking on her?"

"Sure, hon." Mrs. Adler walked down the hall and Maggie swiveled to stare at the front door.

She slowly walked over to it.

The knob jiggled and she stepped back, heart thumping. "Who is it?" She hated the tremble in her voice, but after this morning, the bank robber's threat loomed close to the front of her mind.

The knob stilled. Faint footsteps reached her ears, and she felt her pulse kick it up a notch.

Maggie went to the side window and looked out just I time to see a slim jean-clad figure race around the side of the house.

Slim, tall, ragged, loose-fitting jeans.

Slim? The man from the bank?

Her breath snagged in her throat and fear thumped through her.

Fingers fumbled for the phone. Finally, she wrapped her hand around it then punched in 911.

Reese slapped the pen down onto the desk. He'd prefer to work with a computer, but his hadn't been set up yet. Looking around, he smiled. Not that much different in this office than the one he'd come from. Washington, D.C., was just bigger and louder.

Eli shoved a ragged-looking man in front of him as he escorted him down the hall to the holding cell. The man let loose a string of curses that didn't stop even when the door clanked shut.

Reese's radio crackled on his shoulder.

Nope, not that much different. And maybe just as loud.

He looked at Eli and gestured toward the prisoner. "That Pete?"

"The one and only."

Pete Scoggins. The town drunk. Reese had heard about him five minutes after being in town.

Pete wilted to the floor of the cell and Eli slid into the desk opposite Reese. "Anything on the bank robbery?"

"No. Anything on the identity of the man who cracked his head on the floor?"

Eli shook his head. "He's awake and released from the hospital and into our custody, but he's not talking."

"She said he wouldn't," Reese murmured.

"What's that?"

"Maggie. She said the man wouldn't talk."

Eli blew out a sigh. "Well, she's got it right so far."

"Anything on a gunshot wound coming in at any of the hospitals?"

"Nothing." Eli pursed his lips and ran a hand over his chin. "I've gotten the word out to be on the lookout for the two other robbers, one with a gunshot wound in his shoulder. So far, we're batting zero."

"Hey, I can hear you back here real good," Pete hollered from his cell. "You talking about those boys who robbed the bank, ain't ya?"

Eli rolled his eyes. "Yeah, Pete. We are. We'll try to keep it down so you can sleep it off."

"I seen 'em, you know."

Reese lifted a brow and got up to follow Eli. Eli stood in front of Pete's cell. "Where? What do you know about them?"

Pete yawned and shrugged. "I'll tell you after I get me a good hot meal."

"Aw, you're just yanking my chain," Eli said and turned to go back down the hall. But Reese wasn't so sure.

"Give me something on those guys, and I'll see what I can do about the hot meal."

Pete eyed him. "You're new here."

Reese met his gaze. "I am."

"Don't know if I can trust you." He looked down the hall. "Hey, Eli! This new boy trustworthy?"

"Yep," Eli hollered back.

"Saw 'em in Miz Holly's café eating before the robbery. I was sitting at the counter drinking me a coffee and they were talking real low, but I could hear 'em. I inched over and heard one of 'em say he'd take care of the woman."

The woman. Maggie? Reese's gut clenched. How would they—

The dispatcher's voice came over his radio. "911 call, an intruder at six, seven, zero, Firebird Lane."

Eli frowned and stood, grabbing his keys. "That's Maggie's address."

Reese's heart thudded, his sudden adrenaline rush familiar, pushing his senses to the hyperalert range that had kept him alive more than once. "I know. I just dropped her off."

The two men raced for the door, Eli barking into his radio. "Let her know we're on the way."

"Hey!" Pete hollered. "Don't forget my food!"

The ten-minute drive up the mountain to the clearing that led to the lake seemed to take forever. Reese found himself imagining all sorts of awful things happening. "Do you think he came back?"

Eli didn't ask who he meant. "I don't know. I wouldn't have thought it, but weirder things have happened."

Worry surged through him. Would the bank robber, known only as Slim, have any compunction about hurting a baby? A wave of nausea swept through him at the thought.

"Is she still on the phone?"

Eli relayed the question to the dispatcher then nodded. He shot a glance at Reese. "She said the guy ran off into the woods. He had on baggy jeans and a black T-shirt with short cropped hair."

Reese's jaw tightened. "That's pretty close to how the robbers were dressed. They all had masks on, too."

They finally pulled into the driveway he'd just left about an hour earlier. Deputy Jason White swung in behind them.

On the outside, everything looked fine, peaceful. Undisturbed. But when Maggie opened the door, he could see the strain on her face, the tension in her shoulders.

Climbing out of the car, he and Eli walked up to the porch. She pointed to the back of the house. "He ran that way."

Eli nodded and glanced at Reese. "You stay with her. I'll check it out." He looked at Jason. "You go that way, make a search of the perimeter."

Jason took off.

Reese took her soft hand in his and led her back inside. "Why don't you sit down and tell me what happened."

She dropped onto the couch, leaned her head back and closed her eyes. "I do believe this has been the longest day of my life."

Reese could see her frustration, her fear.

"My husband called. I'm going to have to go." Reese looked up to see a woman standing in the doorway to the den.

Maggie made the introductions. He reached for his radio and said, "Just a minute. I'll get Deputy White to escort you home as soon as he's finished clearing the perimeter of the house. Until we find out the intentions of the person snooping around, I don't want you out there by yourself."

Mrs. Adler nodded, her frown furrowing, the lines in her forehead deep with worry. Five minutes later, in response to Reese's call, Deputy White appeared on the front porch and Reese waved him inside. "Anything?"

Deputy White shook his head. "Nothing that I can see. If someone was here, he's gone now."

"Thanks. Mrs. Adler's ready to go. Do you mind taking her home?"

"Sure, be happy to." The deputy escorted the woman out to his car.

He turned back to Maggie, opened his mouth to question her further—and heard Belle crying.

A low groan slipped from her throat and before he could stop himself, he placed a hand on her shoulder. "I'll get her."

Grateful surprise lit her eyes, and she melted back onto the cushion.

Reese followed the wails down the hall to the nursery. It was tastefully decorated in pink-and-brown polka dots, and he couldn't help but smile.

The smile slipped when he saw the baby standing up, holding on to the railing, staring at him and blinking. A puzzled frown creased her forehead, and she looked as if she might start crying again. "Hey there, Belle. It's all right. It's just me."

His throat tightened as he recognized what he was doing. He was using the same voice he used to—

Oh, God, help me.

What had he been thinking? Volunteering to get the child from her crib. All he could see when he looked at her was his own baby daughter's lifeless face. The last baby he'd held, and she'd been gone. She'd never had a chance to pull in a breath this side of heaven. His hands shook, and he clenched them.

You can do this.

But he wasn't sure he could.

"Reese? Everything okay?" Maggie called from the other room.

He found his voice and some small measure of strength. "Yeah. Just fine."

When Belle's face scrunched up again as if she was getting ready to crank out a cry, he hurried across the room and lifted her from the crib. Her frown stayed as he held her at arm's length straight out in front of him.

And that's the way they walked down the hall into the den.

Belle's head swiveled and when she saw her mother sitting on the couch, her face brightened and she leaned toward her. Reese let her slide from his outstretched grasp into Maggie's embrace.

He backed up and perched on the edge of the recliner, his heart aching, memories fogging his thinking.

"Are you all right?" Maggie asked. She cocked her head, looking at him as though trying to figure out what was going on inside him.

She probably thought he was an idiot, based on how he carried Belle. He clamped down on his emotions and cleared his throat. "Yeah. Sure. I'm fine. I just..." He motioned toward a now-content Belle.

"Don't have much experience with babies?" she asked with a raised brow.

"Ah, no. I don't." Desperate for a change of subject, Reese touched the radio on his shoulder and got Eli. "Anything?"

"Nothing really. I'll be up there in a minute."

True to his word, Eli knocked about a minute later and let himself into the house. Wiping his shoes on the mat, he said, "I found some disturbed ground, but can't tell if it's recent or not."

"Like someone watching the house?" Reese asked.

A pause. "Yeah. Could be. But probably not. I don't think it was the robber."

Reese wasn't sure. "Maybe not. Maybe it was just a teenager or someone looking for an empty place to crash for the night. The more I think about it, the more I don't see how someone could have been waiting for her. How would they know who she was in the first place, much less where she lives?"

Maggie said, "So this was just a random thing? Someone tests the doorknob to see if I'm home and then runs off when I ask who's there?"

Eli sighed. "It could be some high school kids. We have our fair share of troublemakers. Nothing too serious, but…"

Maggie frowned and bounced Belle on her knee.

Reese said, "There hasn't been time for the guy who threatened you to find you. It was just a few hours ago."

"What if he followed us home?" she asked.

Eli and Reese exchanged a glance. "You mean these guys pretended to leave the bank and doubled back to watch the action?"

She shrugged. "Why not?"

Another exchanged glance with Eli and Reese rubbed his chin. "I can't say it's not possible. Highly unlikely, but not impossible." He paused. "Then again, you were really the one who made it possible for us to capture one of them."

She grimaced. "And he did threaten me—us."

Reese looked at Eli. "What do you think?"

Eli pursed his lips. "I think it's too soon to say, but I'd rather be safe than sorry." Reese nodded. Eli then said, "Why don't you keep an eye on things around here just until we know for sure."

"You mean while he's on duty, right?" Maggie asked. She swiveled her head back and forth between the two men. "I mean, I wouldn't expect him to volunteer his time or anything."

Surprisingly enough, the thought of volunteering to spend time with Maggie wasn't a hardship. If only looking at her with the baby didn't send shards of pain shooting through his heart.

"I don't mind. I live just across the lake. If you need me,

just call." It was the least he could do, wasn't it? After all, she'd probably saved him from taking a bullet when she'd pulled the ropes and downed the bank robber who had his gun pointed at Reese.

He pulled out his cell phone. "What's your phone number?"

Maggie rattled it off. He punched it in his phone and soon heard hers ringing. He hung up and said, "Okay, now it's on your phone. Put it on speed dial and use it if you need it."

She bit her lip then said, "I don't want to put you out."

"You're not putting me out, I promise." But the faster he got away from here, the faster he could start figuring out how he was going to handle being around a baby on a regular basis. Because he already knew he wanted to get to know Maggie better.

Belle started squirming and Maggie stood with the infant on her hip. "Then if you don't mind, I'll take you up on the offer." She shot a look at the door. "Because whether you believe it or not, I have a feeling this is only the beginning."

Reese thought about what jailbird Pete had said and had a feeling she was absolutely right.

THREE

Maggie's words echoed in her own ears long after the men left. She shivered, feeling scared and unsafe in the house for the first time since she'd moved in.

Knowing Reese was across the lake helped, but…

She fed Belle supper, played with her until her bedtime, then put her down.

In the quiet darkness, she now had time to think. To process everything that had happened over the course of the day.

As she thought, she checked the locks, tested the doors and peered through the blinds. She left every light outside burning.

Through a small copse of trees, she could see her nearest neighbor's den light burning. Mrs. Adler. Fondness filled her. The woman reminded her very much of her own grandmother, who'd passed away about five years ago. Maggie missed her. Almost as much as she missed her mother.

She'd never known her father.

A fact that weighed heavy on her heart.

While Maggie had had her grandfather the early years of her life, she didn't want Belle growing up with the emptiness of not having a father figure in her life.

With that thought, she slid into the recliner, noticing

the lingering scent of Reese's musky cologne. Drawing in a deep breath, Maggie felt a longing fill her.

And a loneliness.

She wanted someone in her life. Someone to share good times and bad. Someone to share Belle with.

But memories of her husband intruded, filling her with that familiar fear. What if she picked the wrong man again? What if there was something wrong with her judgment meter? She couldn't live through another abusive marriage. And she had more than herself to think of now. She wouldn't make decisions without first considering every consequence.

And why was she even thinking about this anyway?

Lord, we need to talk...

Her phone rang and she rose with a groan to answer it on the third ring. She frowned at the unfamiliar number displayed on her caller ID. "Hello?"

"Maggie, is that you?"

"Shannon?" Her sister-in-law. Her husband, Kent's, only sibling. "How are you? How did you get this number?"

"I'm fine and tracking you down wasn't easy, believe me. What are you doing? Hiding out?"

Guilt stabbed Maggie. She should at least have called Shannon and let her know that she and Belle were okay. "No, not hiding out, just living pretty simple. I'm sorry I haven't called."

"I'm sorry, too. How's my Belle?"

Maggie smiled. One thing for sure, Shannon doted on her niece. "She's fine. Sleeping right now, thank goodness."

"I want to see her. To see you."

Did Maggie want that? As much as Shannon loved Belle, she was also the sister of the man who'd liked to use Maggie as a punching bag. And Shannon had adored her brother, refusing to believe anything bad about him. "I...um..."

"Please, Maggie."

The quiet plea did her in. "Well, I suppose. When would you come?"

"I'm not sure. Let me...check on some things and I'll call you back."

"Okay."

Maggie said goodbye and hung up, her mind spinning, her heart pounding. Shannon had always intimidated Maggie. And Maggie wasn't even sure that she could explain why if someone asked. The woman just seemed to have it all together. At least the world's view of "having it all together." A good job, a nice house and friends who held the same social status.

Social status that Maggie had never had, nor really wanted. And Maggie couldn't help the feeling that Shannon had looked down on her for being a stay-at-home mother.

Even though that's what Kent had insisted she do.

He hadn't wanted her to work, to have any way of being able to support herself. He'd wanted her totally dependent on him. And she'd bought into it for a while. He'd convinced her that he was all she needed. He would take care of her. Something she'd missed since losing each and every family member. But once the abuse started, she knew she had to do something.

She'd had to sneak online classes to keep her teaching certificate current. Though now, thanks to her grandfather, Maggie didn't have to work unless she wanted to.

Which she did. She loved her job.

Loved helping her students and earning a living that allowed her to provide for herself and Belle. The money her grandfather had left her was there if she needed it. Otherwise, it would go to Belle. Satisfaction filled her. Maggie was so grateful she could leave that money to Belle, so the girl wouldn't have to scrape and scrounge and work three jobs while trying to go to school. And she'd never have to be dependent on a man to take care of her. Never.

A scratching at her window made her jerk.

Then a surge of anger flowed hot and heavy through her veins.

Enough was enough.

Reese tossed and turned. At 2:00 a.m., he felt frustrated and tired.

And worried.

Which was why he couldn't sleep.

After taking care of the situation at Maggie's, he'd gone back to Holly's café, ordered the daily special and taken it back to the jail for Pete.

The man looked surprised—and grateful.

Reese felt a twinge of sympathy for the fellow and had a feeling Eli often fed him his only hot meal of the day. He'd interrogated Pete while he wolfed the food down, but Pete had nothing else to add to his previous story.

So now, in the darkness, questions bombarded Reese. Questions about the bank robbery, the man Maggie had seen in her yard and questions about his attraction to a woman with a baby.

He'd promised himself he'd never put his heart on the line again. He'd had his shot at a family and happily-ever-after, and it had been snatched from him when his wife and child had died in childbirth.

So why couldn't he get the pretty mother out of his mind?

Tossing aside the covers, he padded to the window that

overlooked the lake. Peering across, he could see Maggie's house lit up like a Christmas tree.

Realization hit him.

She was all alone and scared. The nights would be the worst. He knew this from experience. She would play the scene from the bank over and over in her mind, building it up, picturing what could have happened instead of what actually had happened. And she would work herself into a ball of nerves and fear. And with the threat the robber left ringing in the air, she would be jumping at every creak and moan of the house, wondering if the man was back to follow through on his promise.

Without a second's hesitation, he picked up his phone and dialed Maggie's number. She might be afraid of the phone ringing at this time of night, but his number and name were programmed in her phone. Once she saw it was him, she would be all right.

"Hello?" Her low, husky voice trembled over him.

"You can't sleep either?" he asked.

She gave a self-conscious little laugh. "I'm assuming you can see my well-lit house?"

"Reminds me of Christmas."

A sigh slipped through the line. "No, I fell asleep for a bit, but then started hearing things."

He frowned. "Hearing things? Like what?"

"Something scraping against my window." Another little laugh escaped her. One that didn't hold much humor. "I was angry enough to chew someone up and spit him out. I went flying out the door and no one was there."

"You did what?" He nearly had a coronary. "Maggie, may I just say that was incredibly stupid?"

"Oh, I know. What was even more stupid was the butcher knife in my hand. I used it cut the branch that was knocking against the window."

Some of his adrenaline slowed. But he still warned her, "Don't ever do anything like that again. Not after today."

She went silent.

He hurried to say, "Not that I have the right to tell you what to do, but—"

"No, you're right." This time her voice was soft. "I know you're right. It was stupid. I just let my fury get the better of me. It's just that the thought of being a victim again—" She stopped. "I won't do that again. I promise."

He felt slightly better. Then frowned as he realized what she'd said. Victim again? Unsettled, he started to ask her about it then stopped. She'd cut off her sentence. He took that to mean she wasn't ready to talk about it.

Instead, he said, "I tell you what. Since I'm going to be awake for the next few hours, I'll keep an eye on your place. You can rest easy."

For a moment she didn't respond. Then her voice, choked with tears or relief, he couldn't tell, reached his ear. "I really hate to say okay, but I…would truly appreciate it. That is, if you're sure you're not going to be sleeping anyway."

He let a sad smile curve his lips. "I'm not."

"Okay, then. I think I'll try to go to bed."

"Sweet dreams, Maggie."

She hung up, and he watched a few of her lights go off. The small manmade lake was probably only half a mile in diameter, but it would only take him about a minute to reach her house by motorcycle or car should he have to do so.

The dark night called to him. Slipping on his heavy coat and a pair of jeans and boots, he walked outside and down to the dock. Sitting there he wondered again at the strange things that had happened to Maggie that day.

And figured he might be losing a lot of sleep in the near future.

* * *

Reese walked into the sheriff's office a little later than usual Tuesday morning. He'd finally gone to sleep around 5:30 a.m. when he'd noticed Maggie up and moving around, her shadow dancing across the window blinds. The bundle in her arms told him Belle was an early riser.

So here he was at nine o'clock instead of his usual eight o'clock. Fortunately, Eli didn't require his deputies to punch a clock. They all worked more than forty hours a week and if one of them needed a little flexibility, as long as someone was willing to stay a little longer on shift to cover, Eli was fine with that.

Reese decided he could learn to like that kind of schedule.

Eli looked up and turned from his computer at Reese's entrance. "You ready to question our prisoner?"

"He lawyer up?"

"Oh, yeah, first chance he got."

Reese shrugged. "Let's have at him then."

"After we take a crack at him, he'll move up to the larger prison in Bryson City where he'll wait to see the judge who'll set bail and all that."

"Where is he?"

"Talking to his lawyer in the holding cell." Eli stood and grabbed a ring of keys, which made Reese grin. In Washington, one simply pressed a button and the door opened. They still used keys here. Eli noticed the look. "We don't have a lot of crime here." He frowned. "Although, I have to say, it seems to be picking up lately." Then he shrugged. "But why spend the money to upgrade?" Eli passed him on the way to the back and said, "I'll get our prisoner and his lawyer and meet you in the interrogation room."

"Sure. Be there in a minute."

Reese noticed the brand-new laptop sitting on his desk and smiled. Now that was more like it.

He booted it up and pulled the sheet of paper from his drawer that had his email address and other pertinent information he needed to do his job here in Rose Mountain.

Setting that aside to deal with later, he headed for the interrogation room.

A bald man in his late forties sat next to his client. Eli and the lawyer seemed to know each other and shook hands. Eli said, "This is Mr. Nathan Forsythe." Reese shook his hand then sat down and crossed his arms. The one thing he really hated about interrogations was giving up his weapon. He felt incomplete without the comforting weight of the gun under his left arm.

Once everyone was settled, the bank robber slouched in his chair, his hard eyes on the table in front of him.

Reese gave him a hard stare. "Hello, Charlie."

The man didn't even look up.

Eli said, "We ran your prints through AFIS. Welcome to Rose Mountain, Mr. John C. Berkley. Looks like you have a pretty nice rap sheet here."

Tension ran through Berkley as he finally lifted his gaze. He drilled Reese with a silent look filled with hate and a cold confidence that made Reese narrow his eyes.

Eli leaned forward. "Now, would you like to tell us who your partners are and where we can find them?"

Without expression, Berkley simply said, "No."

"Of course not." Eli nodded. "Well, then, I guess we'll send you on up to Bryson City. Oh, and I'm going to let it be known that you weren't just bank robbing, you were going after a baby."

That got Berkley's attention. His shoulders straightened and the surly attitude slid off his face. "Wait a minute, that's not true. You can't do that."

Eli shrugged and Reese admired the man's acting abilities. "I think it is true. What do you think, Reese?"

Reese rubbed his chin as though pondering Eli's question. "He told her to come with him. She had a baby she wasn't leaving behind. Yeah, at least attempted kidnapping." Reese kept his voice casual, as though he didn't have a care in the world. "Especially since we have someone who witnessed you saying something about 'The woman is mine.' Now, which woman were you talking about? There were only three in the bank."

Berkley's eyes narrowed. "I don't know what you're talking about."

"I don't believe you, but we can come back to that. I'm real interested in the fact that you didn't mind putting a child at risk and attempting to kidnap her mother. That might not go over so well in some prisons."

Berkley fidgeted, and Reese could tell he was working hard to keep himself under control.

Eli pressed the issue. "Lots of guys in prison, especially those with families of their own, don't take kindly to those who put children in danger—you know what I'm saying?"

A bead of sweat dripped from Berkley's forehead. He knew.

But he clamped his lips shut and looked at his lawyer, who said, "Don't say anything. I'll see what we can do with the judge." Forsythe nailed Eli and Reese with a glare. "That's pretty low, Eli."

"So is trying to rob my town's bank and kidnap a local resident." Eli stood and walked to the door.

Reese leaned forward toward Berkley, knuckles resting on the table. "And so is trying to shoot me. That tends to make me a little angry."

Barkley said nothing, just met Reese stare for stare.

Then a slow smile slipped over the man's face, and he leaned back in his chair.

Reese stood, hoping his contempt for the man was obvious. As he walked toward the door, Berkley gave a low chuckle. "You think you know everything don't you, Kirkpatrick?"

Reese paused, exchanged a glance with Eli and the silent lawyer. "What do you mean?"

"I don't mean anything." He looked at his lawyer. "Get me out of here."

Reese stepped in front of them. "*What* do you mean?"

For a moment the man simply stared at him, then sneered, "I *mean,* your little lady messed up when she decided to mess with our job. She'd better watch her back cuz this ain't over."

FOUR

Reese felt his blood boil as he watched Eli escort Berkley from the room. Was the man all talk? Or was there more to this than met the eye? Berkley's attitude suggested that he knew something they didn't, and it made Reese's palms itch. He wanted to watch the bank video, see if anything struck him.

Eli had said it was being sent over. So he'd wait for it.

He dialed Maggie's number and it went to voice mail. Then he dialed Mitchell's, the other deputy on duty.

"Mitchell here."

"This is Reese. What's your location?"

"I'm just on the edge of town, at the base of the mountain."

"Will you swing by Maggie Bennett's place?" He gave him the address. "Just check and make sure everything's all right?"

"Sure."

Reese's stomach rumbled, and he frowned. Although he felt better about sending Mitchell to check on Maggie, he couldn't help remembering Berkley's words. "It's not over yet." And why would one of the robbers talk about "the woman" being his *before* the robbery? Had Pete gotten his conversations mixed up? If not, which woman? One of the tellers?

Maggie?

But Maggie's trip to the bank had been spur of the moment. Hadn't it?

His stomach sent up hunger signals once again and Reese sighed. He'd grab a quick bite then get back to work. He'd left in a hurry this morning, which meant he hadn't taken the time to eat breakfast.

Reese headed for the door. "Hey, wait up." Eli came from the back. "Where you headed?"

"Thought I'd grab a biscuit at the diner. I missed breakfast."

"You mind if I come along? White's got the jail covered, and Alice is on the phones." Alice Colby, the department secretary, was a pleasant woman in her early fifties. She had salt-and-pepper-colored hair and blue eyes that sparkled all the time. Reese liked her. Jason White was the new hire who'd started the same day as Reese. Reese didn't like him as much as he liked Alice. But the deputy was competent, and Reese knew Eli was glad to have a full staff once again.

"Sure, come on," he said. "What's wrong? Holly didn't feed you this morning?"

Eli grinned. "Not this morning. Holly's not feeling all that great."

"Why does that put a smile on your face?"

"She'll feel better in a few weeks. After the first trimester."

"First tri— Oh." Holly was pregnant. A pang shot through him, and grief hit him in the gut. Covering the split-second reaction, Reese cleared his throat. "Ah, well, congratulations."

The smile slipped from Eli's face. "I'm sorry."

"For what?" Reese forced a lightness into his voice that he didn't feel.

"It still hits hard, doesn't it?"

Reese didn't bother to try to avoid the question. "Yeah. It does. Not as hard as it used to, so time's helping, but it still hurts." This time his smile was real. "But I'm happy for you and Holly. That's great. I hope it's a girl for her sake, though. Even things out with you males in the family."

Eli slapped him on the back and gave his shoulder a friendly squeeze. "Me, too. Come on, I'm starving. Let's eat while we have a chance."

On the way to the diner, Eli stopped residents of the town and introduced Reese to each one. Friendly faces welcomed him, and Reese felt a small sliver of peace slide into his heart.

Coming to Rose Mountain had been the best choice he'd made in a long time.

"By the way, don't forget about the church potluck dinner Wednesday night. When I was a bachelor, I looked forward to those things like a kid does Christmas. Best home cooking you'll find."

Reese nodded and smiled. "I heard the announcement in church last Sunday." One thing he'd done as soon as he'd moved to town was find a church. He'd settled into his house on Saturday a week ago and gotten up and gone to church with Eli and Holly and Cal and Abby the next morning.

He wondered if Maggie Bennett would be there.

When he walked into the diner, his eyes landed on the woman his thoughts couldn't seem to stay away from. Belle sat in her lap, picking Cheerios out of Maggie's hand and eating them one by one. Like a homing pigeon, he made his way to her, drawn by her deep brown eyes. He was vaguely aware of Eli following along behind. She smiled when she saw him. "Good morning, Reese."

"Morning. How'd you sleep last night?"

"Pretty well, thanks to you. Knowing you were watching was—well, it made a big difference. Thanks."

He returned her smile. "It was no problem."

Eli cleared his throat, and Maggie looked past him to greet the man. "Hi, Eli."

"Maggie. No classes this morning?"

"Not until 11:00 today. I started on paperwork about 6:00 this morning and decided I had definitely earned a break. So here we are."

Reese thought about that question he'd wanted to ask her. "Hey, do you go to the bank every Monday?"

She lifted a brow at him. "Yes. Usually. I get paid by electronic deposit on a weekly basis. I go to get my cash for the week and then go to the different places to pay my bills."

"You don't use checks? Pay online?"

She shook her head. "No. I do it this way on purpose. It gets me out of the house. I spend many hours online with my job." She shrugged. "I could do everything online, but I like getting out, visiting with people and…" She flushed. "I know it sounds silly. I just need that personal interaction."

"It doesn't sound silly," he reassured her. He understood what she was saying, and his mind was already clicking through what it meant.

Belle jabbered at Reese and held her arms out to him. He backpedaled, almost knocking Eli over. Maggie jerked and lifted a brow at him. Feeling like a fool, he stammered, "Um, well, I guess we'd better get a table. See you."

He turned and headed for the table in the far corner, feeling Maggie's puzzled gaze follow him until he was able to slide into the seat and out of her line of sight.

Eli seated himself on the opposite side and shook his head. "What in the world was that?"

A cold sweat broke across Reese's brow and he closed his eyes on a groan. "I don't know. I'm an idiot."

"Have you talked to anyone about this? Like a professional counselor?"

Eli's soft question sent darts through Reese's heart. "Yeah. I did."

"And?"

"It helped, but..."

"The grief is still there. And it will be for the rest of your life, I know, but..."

Guilt shook him. He opened his eyes and looked straight into Eli's compassionate gaze. "For Keira, the grief is less sharp. It's more of a sadness for what could have been, the loss of what we had. I miss her. A lot. And I'm sorry she died. I wish I could change that, but I can't." He sighed. "It's hard to admit it, but I'm ready to move on. To find someone to spend the rest of my life with. But..."

"But?"

"When it comes to babies, I just... It's hard. I don't know why it's so hard." Frustration at his inability to put his feelings into words washed over him. "It just is. And I need to find a way to move on, to accept the loss and deal with it, but..."

"You lost your wife and daughter, Reese. That's huge."

Reese swallowed against the lump in his throat. "I know." He stirred in his seat, restless with the direction of the conversation. Fortunately, the waitress arrived before he had to contribute further to it.

Then Eli changed the subject. "What was that about? Maggie and her trips to the bank?"

"She has a routine. A routine someone has figured out in her short time here in Rose Mountain."

Eli nodded, knowledge lighting his eyes. "And they hit the bank at the time she was going to be there. Just as she was every Monday."

"Coincidence?"

"Maybe."

"But you don't think so?"

"I think time will tell. I also think we need to keep a really close eye on her."

Reese stared at the woman who'd already made such an impression on his heart. "I don't think I'm going to mind that." He also wouldn't mind finding out exactly why the pretty mother came to be in the wrong place at the wrong time.

In fact, finding that out might require spending a lot of time with her and getting to know her better.

He couldn't help the small smile that slipped across his lips.

Maggie pushed the sippy cup from Belle's grasping fingers, tired of the "throw it on the floor so Mommy can pick it up" game.

Belle protested with a loud squeal so Maggie stood, trying to juggle the baby, her purse and the diaper bag. Her wallet fell to the floor when it tipped out of her tilted purse.

With Belle on her hip, she squatted, attempting to keep her balance while she retrieved the wallet.

"Let me hold her a minute."

Maggie looked up to see Mrs. Adler standing behind her. Belle grinned when she saw her.

Grateful for the woman's intervention, Maggie handed Belle over. While Belle grabbed a handful of Mrs. Adler's graying shoulder-length hair and tried to get it in her mouth, Maggie picked up her wallet.

When she stood again, she nearly mashed her nose into the uniform-covered broad chest. "Oh!"

Reese's strong hands came up to grasp her upper arms, and she shivered at the contact. He gave her a crooked smile that didn't match the look in his eyes. He handed her a dusty pacifier. "This fell out of your purse and bounced almost to my table. Would hate for you to need it and it not be there."

Maggie took it from him and stepped back to catch her breath. Being so close to him did crazy things to her pulse. She swallowed hard. "Thanks."

"No problem." He smiled at Mrs. Adler. "Good to see you, ma'am."

"And you, Deputy Kirkpatrick."

He smiled. "You can call me Reese."

Reese returned to his seat, and Maggie tucked the dirty pacifier in her purse to wash later. As Reese settled himself onto the plastic-covered seat, she saw Eli raise a brow at his new hire.

The flush on Reese's cheeks made her wonder if perhaps she triggered the same crazy feelings in him that he did in her.

While thankful for the return of the pacifier, she still frowned as she watched the two men engage in conversation. Because while Deputy Reese Kirkpatrick seemed to have a soft spot for her, she couldn't help but notice that when he offered her the pacifier and addressed Mrs. Adler, he never once looked at Belle.

In the small bedroom that served as her office, Maggie clicked out of her virtual classroom and took her headphones off. She was pleased with the five students who had shown up, and the class had gone well. In fact, all her classes this morning had had lively discussions and productive work. Satisfaction filled her.

Mrs. Adler entertained Belle in the den while Maggie worked. Now that Belle was getting older, Maggie needed someone to help out during her class times and for four hours a day, four days a week, Mrs. Adler was happy to do it. Not only that, the woman liked to cook. She seemed to feel as if it was her personal duty to keep Maggie in casseroles and pies. Maggie didn't argue with her.

She pictured the food-laden tables she knew would be spread out tomorrow night in the church gym and her stomach growled. The sandwich she'd downed in a hurry a couple of hours ago had worn off. She'd find a snack in a minute. Right now, she had something on her mind and needed to think a bit.

Maggie got up and walked toward the closet where she had a small portable file box. As she passed the window, movement caught her eye.

Stopping, she glanced out. The bedroom was in the back corner of the house. The view from the window was part lake to her right and part woods to her left. The sheer curtains allowed light to flood the room during the day. But now, Maggie wished she had something heavier and more concealing over the windows. She shivered and waited. Watching. Her mind flashed to the robber's threat that he would kill her.

Would he really? She remembered the look in his eye as he spewed the threat and decided, yes, he really would.

Fear trembled through her and she pulled in a deep breath. For the next few minutes, she simply stood and watched the area outside the window, then she moved to Belle's room and looked out. Again, she saw nothing that caused her concern. Before she left Belle's room, she checked the window latch. It was fastened securely.

Feeling a bit better, thinking it was just an animal or something that had captured her attention, she let herself relax slightly. Returning to her office, she went straight to the closet. The file box she wanted sat on the top shelf.

Maggie pulled it down and brought it to the desk.

Before she went any further, she couldn't resist one more glance out the window.

Nothing.

She turned back to the box, opened the latch and lifted the lid. Ever since the attempted bank robbery, she'd been troubled by the fact that she could have been killed. She wasn't ready to die, of course, but it wasn't so much the act of dying as it was dying and leaving Belle to face the world without her.

Maggie sorted through the files until she came to the one she wanted. The one marked WILL. When she'd lived with her husband, she'd learned fast to hide things she didn't want him to know about. He was suspicious and mean and went through her things often, accusing her of hiding money from him.

Guilt pulled at her. Well, he'd been right about that. She'd been hiding things from him. She'd been planning her escape from the man for several months because she knew if she didn't get away from him, she would eventually wind up dead. And now she had more than herself to think of. She had to take care of Belle.

Maggie pulled the one sheet of paper labeled LAST WILL AND TESTAMENT from the file, sat in the chair and simply looked at it. She really had to do something about guardianship for Belle in case something happened to her. The attempted bank robbery yesterday had hit home the fact that Maggie had no other living relatives. None.

Except for her deceased husband's sister, Shannon Bennett. And she wasn't even a blood relative. The woman was thirty-seven years old, had never married and seemed to prefer it that way. She was listed as the person who would get custody of Belle in the event of Maggie's death. And while Maggie knew without a doubt that Shannon was crazy about Belle, that she would take care of her, provide for her and love her, Maggie hesitated. She just wasn't sure she wanted to leave Belle with her. For a number of reasons.

The doorbell rang and she jumped.

Mrs. Adler called, "I'll get it."

Maggie relaxed and went back to trying to make a decision about what to do about Belle in the event of her death. Not something she planned on happening, but the bank robbery still had her shaken.

A high-pitched scream echoed through the house. Maggie jerked, bolted to her feet and raced down the short hall to find the woman standing in the doorway, hands clasped to her mouth.

"What is it?" Maggie's heart thudded as she stepped around Mrs. Adler and stared down at the dead squirrel on her porch. He lay on his back, feet in the air.

The words painted in red next to him read, "You're next."

FIVE

Maggie's shaky phone call still echoed in his mind as Reese stood on the porch looking down at the dead animal. The bright sun in the blue cloudless sky cast a cheery glow around him. A direct contrast to the chilling message next to the carcass.

Eli stepped forward and placed a hand on Mrs. Adler's shoulder. The woman still trembled as she twisted a tissue between her fingers. "Let me call Jim to come get you," Eli offered.

"No, I have my car. I'll be fine." She bit her lip. "I'd rather he not know about this. We're going to Asheville day after tomorrow for some heart tests. This wouldn't be good for him."

"I'm so sorry," Maggie whispered, her face pale and drawn.

Mrs. Adler reached over and took Maggie's hand in hers. "It's not your fault, honey. Someone is just getting his kicks in a twisted way." She fluttered her hand as though to say she was going to try to ignore it.

Reese wished he could.

But the would-be bank robber's threats still rang in his ears. He hadn't thought the two who'd escaped would have hung around the area. But maybe one had revenge on his mind. Maybe the person Maggie saw running from her home yesterday had indeed been the robber who'd threatened them. But why go after Maggie? Reese was the one who'd shot him.

Then again, if Maggie hadn't pulled the rope, everything would have ended differently. They would have gotten away with their money and Slim wouldn't have a bullet hole in him.

Eli looked up from the squirrel. "He was already dead. Been dead a couple of days, I'd say. Our joker probably came across him and decided it'd be a good way to scare Maggie."

She grunted. "It worked."

"Where's Belle?" Eli asked.

"In her playpen." Maggie glanced through the door and into the den. "She's content right now."

Eli looked at Mitchell, one of his deputies. "Anything on that red substance?"

"It's not blood." He held up the cotton swab he'd used to test the writing. "Maybe paint or some kind of marker."

"Let's get all this stuff bagged." He looked at Maggie. "We'll have to send it off to the lab in Asheville. It may take a while to hear back."

She nodded and ran a hand through her blond hair. She looked tired, the gray smudges under her eyes attesting to the fact that she hadn't gotten much sleep since the robbery. She asked, "What do I do now? If this person is determined to get to me, how do Belle and I—" she shot a glance at Mrs. Adler "—and everyone else in my life, stay safe?"

Reese's jaw firmed. "I live right across the lake, so I can help keep an eye on things." He looked at Eli. "Would it be possible to have deputies on duty drive by every couple of hours for the next few days?"

Eli blew out a sigh and was quiet while he thought about

it. Then he said, "Fortunately, we're not short-staffed any-more. At least we won't be when Cal and Abby get back from Washington. They're due home any time now." Reese nodded. Cal McIvers was also a deputy on the small Rose Mountain police force. Abby, Cal's wife, was Reese's former sister-in-law. Their unconditional love and support had been instrumental in influencing his move to the mountain.

"That'll help."

Eli pulled out his notebook again and wrote as he spoke. "I'll set up a schedule for the drive-bys." He looked at Maggie. "And we can set up a check-in schedule for you."

"What's that?" she asked.

"You call either Reese or me throughout the day at designated times to let us know you're all right. It doesn't have to take long, just a simple, 'I'm fine.'"

Reese nodded. "She can call me." He looked into her eyes. "I'll be available, day or night. If you even feel uneasy, call."

He saw her throat work, the protest form on her lips. Before she could utter a word, he stated firmly, "It's not an imposition. Let me do this. If something happened to you—or Belle—I'd…probably blame myself for letting you talk me out of it. So let's just save me the guilt, okay?"

"Let him do it, honey," Mrs. Adler chimed in. "With the crazy stuff happening in this town lately, it wouldn't hurt." She shook her head. "First Eli has to take over for a crooked sheriff, then drugs being funneled through the elementary school then someone chasing down that sweet Abby McIvers and trying to kill her…" The woman trailed off, her muttered words making Reese wince.

He'd been part of Abby O'Sullivan McIvers's grief. His sister-in-law. He'd blamed her for his wife and daughter's deaths and she'd run from him. Straight to Rose Mountain, where she'd met and married Cal McIvers, one of

Rose Mountain's deputies. Now she had a flourishing pediatric medical practice and the residents of Rose Mountain kept her busy enough that she'd started looking for a partner. Thankfully, Reese had been able to be friendly with her and Cal.

Maggie looked confused. "Dr. Abby?" So she hadn't heard the story of how he'd come to Rose Mountain.

He nodded. "Yes."

Before Mrs. Adler could add to her dialogue about all the bad things happening recently on the mountain, a cry sounded from inside the house.

Belle.

Maggie darted inside while Eli walked Mrs. Adler to her car. "Why don't you call it a day?"

"I believe I will." She climbed in and drove down the drive that would lead her to the two-lane mountain road.

Reese watched her go. The storm door squeaked open and Maggie stepped outside with Belle on her hip.

His heart flipped then settled.

Why was he reacting this way? He hadn't felt anything like attraction for a woman since Keira's death. And now this. He was developing feelings for the mother of a baby. He shook his head at himself and decided he'd better focus on her safety and not the fact that he wanted to push aside his insecurities and fears and lose himself in the possibility that God might have something planned for him and Maggie.

The thought was almost too much right now and something he would have to take the time to think about later.

Belle babbled, and Reese reached out to touch her cheek. When she grinned, he found himself smiling back. Then the sadness hit him once again. But the surprise in Maggie's gaze and the warmth that filled her eyes at his gesture helped ease the grief.

And he wasn't sure what to do about that, either.

"Reese?"

He spun to see Eli standing beside his cruiser. "Yeah?"

"I'm going to see how backed up the lab is." His gaze darted between Maggie and Reese. "Why don't you hang around here for a while and make sure everything's all right."

"Sure, I can do that." Reese felt the heat at the back of his neck and cleared his throat.

Maggie said, "Thanks, Eli."

"Anytime." Everyone cleared out and the sudden silence echoed around them.

Then Maggie nodded toward the door. "Come on in. I was just going to fix some lunch. You hungry?"

"I could eat."

She smiled. "Then let's see what we're having. I don't have another class for two hours. I can catch up on the paperwork tonight." She smirked. "Or at least attempt to. I honestly don't think I'll ever be caught up."

Thunder rumbled in the distance and he looked over his shoulder at the sky as he followed her inside. "It's going to rain tonight. You don't have to go anywhere tomorrow morning, do you?"

"No, why?"

"Because there'll be ice on the roads."

"Oh. No. I'll be right here teaching my classes. Mrs. Adler usually walks over, though. I'll give her a call and warn her not to come if it's icy. For her to fall is the last thing she and her husband need right now." She placed Belle in the high chair and gave her some Cheerios.

Reese stood awkwardly in the doorway. "What can I do to help?"

She studied him for a moment as though weighing

whether or not he really wanted to help. "Do you like salad?"

"If it's got meat on it."

She laughed. "A chef salad it is, then."

He got the lettuce from the fridge and found ham, turkey and all the trimmings for an excellent salad. While Maggie sliced and buttered bread, Belle watched him with curious eyes.

And he found himself returning her stare, wondering what his little girl would have looked like if she'd lived. She would have been almost two years old by now. Biting his lip against the sharp slice of pain, he turned back to chopping the lettuce.

Maggie said, "It's weird having help in the kitchen, but you don't get in the way."

His pain faded and he grinned. "I love to work in the kitchen. Cooking, grilling…" He shrugged. "I like to eat good food and since I'm on my own, I'm responsible for it."

"Where'd you learn to cook?"

Maggie set the two large bowls of salad on the table while he grabbed the dressing and the jug of tea she'd pulled from the fridge. "Will you hand me those two jars of baby food by the microwave?"

He did and they settled down at the table with Maggie seated next to Belle so she could feed her daughter while she ate her own meal.

He blurted out, "I…grew up in foster homes."

She started and stared at him. "Oh. I didn't realize…"

He shrugged. "It's all right. In one of the homes, my foster mother was a gourmet chef." A smile curved his lips as he remembered. "She used to let me help her in the kitchen, and she taught me the ins and outs of cooking."

"How long were you there?"

His smile faded. "Long enough to get attached. Then my

foster father died suddenly, and my foster mother sort of fell apart." He cleared his throat. "But it was a good place for about three years. I think I stayed there from the time I was fourteen until I turned seventeen. After that, the state sent me to live with a family who were nice enough, but it was clear that as soon as I was eighteen and finished with high school, I was on my own. After graduation, I joined the army. They paid for my college."

"How old are you?" she asked as she spooned another small glob of something green in Belle's waiting mouth.

He grimaced and answered, "Thirty-three."

Maggie caught his look and grinned. "I know it looks gross, but she likes it." After another spoonful and a bite of her salad, she asked, "And when you got out of the service, you decided to become a detective?"

He took a sip of tea and nodded. "Well, a cop first, then a detective."

"Why are you here in Rose Mountain, Reese? A big-city detective doesn't just one day decide to move to a small mountain town and become a deputy. It doesn't make sense."

He froze. But she deserved an answer. "I…was going through a tough time when Eli called and asked if I was interested in the job." Sympathy flashed in her pretty eyes, compelling him to tell her, "My wife and—" He let his gaze land on Belle and couldn't form the words. "My wife died about eighteen months ago."

She gasped. "Oh! I'm so sorry."

He blew out a breath. "After that, I sort of fell apart. I needed a change of pace. When Eli called, it was like a gift. I packed up and haven't looked back." At least not on purpose.

Belle thumped her cup on her tray and he flinched. The sippy cup spun on the edge then hit the floor. Belle let out a squeal. He bent to pick up the cup the same time Maggie did and they knocked heads.

Maggie yelped and jerked away from him.

Reese saw stars for a moment then turned his concern to her. "Hey, I'm sorry. Are you all right?"

Maggie held a hand to her head and he reached up to touch the small knot forming on her forehead. She opened her eyes and tears hovered on the edge. She blinked them back and gave a watery laugh. "Sorry, I don't know why I'm crying, but that stung a bit."

He winced. "I know. If I didn't want to permanently alter your perception of me as the tough cop, I'd shed a few tears myself."

That made her laugh and his heart twisted at the sound. He slid his hand from her small wound to cup her cheek. "You should do that more often."

Maggie's breath caught in her throat, and she stared up into his eyes that seemed so deep, if she wasn't careful, she'd find herself drowning in them. She swallowed hard. "What's that?"

"Laugh."

"Oh." She moved away from his touch and handed the cup back to the squirming, cranky Belle.

Who promptly tossed it across the kitchen.

Maggie pulled her child from the high chair and said, "It's nap time, I do believe."

"I guess I should leave." He looked at his watch.

Fear immediately settled around her like a wet blanket on a cold day. Unwanted and uncomfortable. She wanted to toss the fear aside, but wasn't sure how to go about doing that. She forced a smile. "Thanks for coming to the rescue."

Reese nodded and paced to the front door. "You know,

why don't you put her down and I'll just hang around a few more minutes."

Relief slid over her, but she said, "Sometimes she's hard to get down. I might be a little while."

He pulled out his phone. "I can answer a few emails. It's no problem. I want to talk to you about some safety concerns."

So that's why he was offering to stay. Well, whatever the reason, she was glad. She hurried down the hall and into Belle's little room, which she'd decorated with such care. Kent, her husband, hadn't wanted Belle. And he sure hadn't wanted Maggie to spend time and money on decorating a nursery.

A shudder ripped through her as she remembered his violent anger when she'd told him she was pregnant.

Belle yawned and settled her head on Maggie's shoulder. That simple action by her sweet baby settled Maggie's nerves as she lowered herself into the rocker. Usually this was her favorite time of the day, rocking the child, but she now wanted Belle to hurry up and go to sleep. Her mind clicked as she wondered what Reese wanted to talk about. The fact that he'd been open with her and had discussed the loss of his wife was touching. Sympathy made her ache. They'd both lost a spouse.

Only Reese had loved his wife.

By the time Kent had died, the only things Maggie had felt for him were hate and fear.

And then she couldn't help wondering what it would be like to be loved by a man like Reese Kirkpatrick.

SIX

Reese couldn't get Maggie off his mind. Not just because she was a lovely woman, but because she was a lovely woman who was in danger. The menacing message left on her porch drove that home to him, and he felt a responsibility to do something about it.

Reese pulled out the small notebook and pen that he carried everywhere. He started in the den and made notes about the location of the windows and the way the furniture was arranged. Then he moved on to the kitchen.

When he reached her office, he paused, wondering if he should ask permission to invade her space.

"Reese?"

At her quiet voice, he turned. The questioning look in her eyes had him flushing. "Hey." He held up his notebook. "I'm making some notes."

"On what?"

"On how to get you some security around here." He nodded to her office. "Do you mind if I take a look?"

"No, I don't mind. Go ahead."

"You need a security system." He looked at her. "I know they're kind of expensive, but I'll check with Eli and see if he knows someone who could give you a good deal along with excellent security."

Maggie gave a slow nod. "You're right. A security system would help me feel much safer."

"Also, you need motion sensors outside. I can put those up later tonight after I finish my shift." He could feel her eyes on him, watching him. He fidgeted, her fixed gaze making him a little uneasy. "What is it?"

"Why are you doing this? I don't think most deputies would take such an...interest in a victim."

But she wasn't just a victim to him. She was—well, he wasn't sure what she was to him yet, but it was more than a victim. "Because...I want to. Maybe it's because I was in the bank with you." Maybe it's because he was attracted to her and was trying to figure out his confusion about that fact. But one thing was certain. "None of this is your fault, and you shouldn't have to be afraid."

She bit her lip and looked at the floor. "If he really wants to get to me, he will."

Reese felt his jaw go tight. Reaching out, he lifted her chin to look into her eyes. "Don't think like that. We're going to do everything we can to keep you and Belle safe."

He wondered if his determination to succeed in that was a matter of leftover guilt that he hadn't been able to do anything for his wife or baby. His complete and total helplessness in the face of their deaths.

Probably.

But Maggie needed him, and he was going to be there for her.

Her eyes flickered and she swallowed hard as she gave a short nod. "Okay," she whispered.

"Okay." He walked past her into the master bedroom. His first thought was: peace. The room was tasteful, warm and feminine. She'd done the room with colors that reminded him of peaches and cream, and he suddenly felt like a blundering intruder. He made his notes fast from the door. She said, "The window is stuck. I've tried to get it open, but short of using a crowbar, I think it's pretty secure."

He gestured to it. "May I?"

She frowned, but nodded. "Sure."

Reese walked over to the window and pushed the curtains aside. Two quick, sharp tugs and the window slid up.

Lightning flashed, the sound of rain pounding the earth filled his ears. Cold air rushed in, and he quickly shut the window. Over his shoulder, he said, "I think we'll add this window to the list."

She stared, the nonplussed expression on her face almost making him smile in spite of the reason for checking the window. "I guess I need to start working out," she said.

Before he could stop the words, he heard himself saying, "You're perfect just the way you are."

She flushed and cleared her throat as she walked toward him, then past him and into the hall. "You've been in Belle's room, so you know what it looks like."

"I think I've got everything I need." He paused. "I hate to ask this, but what kind of price range is doable for you?"

She tilted her head and shrugged. "It doesn't matter—" Maggie paused, then sighed. "Why don't you get me a couple of quotes, and I'll pick one."

Reese nodded. "I can do that." And then he'd make up the difference if he had to. She was going to have whatever security system it took to keep her safe. And give him a little peace of mind.

Later that afternoon, after Reese left with promises to check on her often and be back to install the motion sensors, Belle played in the playpen while Maggie tried to make a decision about her will. Flashes of the robbery danced across her mind, and she shuddered and tried to force the remembered terror away.

Maggie looked at the balance on the statement from her bank. She still couldn't believe her grandfather had left that much money for Belle.

All the time she'd been under Kent's thumb, been his prisoner in his beautiful house, she'd been so isolated, so afraid to make the wrong move, say the wrong thing or cook the wrong meal.

And getting a job wasn't even an option. A stockbroker, Kent had at first declared he didn't want his wife working because it would make him look unsuccessful, as if he couldn't take care of his own family. Later, Maggie realized it was just another way for him to control her. If he could have found a way to climb inside her mind and take over her thoughts, he would have.

But now she didn't have to worry about that.

There was something about making her own money to pay the bills, to take care of Belle and herself. She felt independent. Free in a way she hadn't been since childhood.

She put the bank statement into the file box and looked at the picture on her desk. Her grandfather and her mother stood arm in arm, smiling as if they didn't have a care in the world.

She missed them. Her grandfather had his faults, but he had loved Maggie.

She thought of the man who'd divorced her grandmother for another woman. "He's a hard, bitter man," her grandmother had told her. Her grandmother had gone to her grave praying for the man who'd hurt her so.

But Maggie had a different memory of her grandfather. She couldn't reconcile the man her grandmother described with the man she'd known the first eleven years of her life. The one who'd taken her for ice cream sundaes and walks in the park. The one who'd nursed her through the flu while her grandmother and mother had to work.

Maggie thought about all the people she knew—people she'd only met since coming to Rose Mountain. And made her decision.

Quickly, she pulled up the template on the computer and started working. Within minutes, she was finished, had the document printed and ready to mail to her lawyer, a nice man she'd met at church. He also represented Eli and Holly. Once done, she stared at the envelope and felt peace flood her. It was the right decision. She slid it under the heavy horse-head paperweight to the right of her computer and made a mental note to mail the envelope tomorrow when she didn't have to walk to the mailbox in the rain.

A knock on the door startled her. She hadn't heard a car drive up. Her eyes flashed to the knives on the kitchen counter, the heavy frying pan on the stove. Her fingers gripped the cordless phone, and she started to dial 911. Then realized if the person meant her harm, he probably wouldn't knock on the door.

Probably.

Although, he didn't seem to have a problem ringing the bell after leaving the dead squirrel and horrible message on the porch.

At the window, she glanced out and breathed a small sigh of relief when she saw Abby McIvers standing on her front porch. Then she frowned. What was she doing here?

Maggie opened the door. "Hello, Dr. McIvers."

The pretty woman smiled. "Please, call me Abby."

The rain slowed to a drizzle as Maggie motioned for her to come in. Abby stepped inside and shrugged out of her heavy winter raincoat. Maggie hung it on the hook beside the door and said, "Come into the den and sit down. What brings you by?" She glanced at the clock and figured she had about twenty minutes before Belle would demand her attention.

"I came to see a patient of mine who lives about three doors down from you. Susan Evans." Abby frowned as she sat on the sofa. "She's due any day now and is scared to death. I told her I'd come out and see her as often as I could." Abby's frown lifted into a smile. "I've heard a lot about you lately from Eli and Reese, and thought I'd come get to know you a bit better."

"A rainy day is always a perfect time for a visit," Maggie said. "Let me put on some coffee."

Abby followed her into the kitchen. "I noticed the police car outside. Cal told me what happened with the robber who escaped, so I'm glad they're keeping an eye on you. I'm sure the attempted bank robbery was incredibly scary."

"Very," Maggie agreed with a shudder.

"So I'll change the subject. How's Belle doing?"

"All recovered from her ear infection, thanks." Belle had suffered her fourth ear infection two weeks ago. Abby had been the physician who'd prescribed the antibiotics and numbing drops. "You saved my sanity. Belle finally fell asleep when we got home, and so did I. We both slept for eight hours straight." She measured the grounds and poured them into the filter.

Abby sat at the table. "I'm glad." A slight pause, then, "Reese thinks a lot of you."

Maggie looked at the woman out of the corner of her eye. "And you think a lot of Reese, don't you?"

A smile curved Abby's lips. "He's become one of Cal's best friends. He's my brother-in-law. Or former brother-in-law."

Maggie jerked. "That's something I didn't know."

"He was married to my sister, Keira."

"He told me she died." Maggie pulled two mugs from the cabinet. Then looked Abby in the eye. "I'm sorry."

Abby's smile turned sad. "I am, too." Then she sighed and her expression turned thoughtful. "It's been a year and a half, though, and I think he's ready to move on."

"Move on?"

The coffee finished brewing and Maggie rose to pour it into the waiting mugs. She handed one to Abby and motioned to the cream and sugar in the middle of the table.

While Abby spooned two heaping teaspoons of sugar, Maggie tried to figure out where the woman was going with this conversation.

Abby picked up where she left off. "Yes, move on. Find someone to spend the rest of his life with."

The speculative look in Abby's eyes caused Maggie to give a nervous laugh. "He and I just met, Abby. I think you might be rushing things a bit here."

"True, I probably am." She shrugged. "I just care about Reese and want to see him happy. And you're the first person he's—"

Maggie waited for Abby to finish. When she didn't, Maggie prompted, "He's what?"

Another shrug, another sip. "Expressed any interest in since my sister died." Her forehead creased. "At least as far as I know. He just moved here from Washington, D.C., about a week ago." She set her cup on the table. "But we've kept in touch on a regular basis and he's come to visit and stay with us a lot over the past year or so whenever he could get time off. Cal and I could tell he was looking for something different." She smiled. "Rose Mountain had gotten to him. He couldn't stay away. And now, according to Cal, Reese can't seem to stay away from you, either."

Maggie shifted, uncomfortable. "Reese is concerned that I might be in danger—that's all it is. And I don't know that I'm ready for any kind of relationship with anyone anyway. I don't have a very good track record with men, and don't know that I trust my judgment anymore."

Sympathy flashed on Abby's face. "Sounds like you have a story to tell."

"Maybe one day." Spilling her guts to a stranger wasn't in her. But she already liked Abby and had a feeling they could become close friends.

Belle's cry came right on schedule. "Excuse me a minute."

"I need to get going anyway. Thanks for the coffee." Abby smiled as she rose and placed her half-finished cup in the sink. "Maybe we can do this again when I can stay longer? Or maybe you and Belle can come out for dinner one night?"

"I'd like that." And she would. She needed a friend here in Rose Mountain. It was time to start trusting people again.

Abby rested a hand on Maggie's upper arm and said, "I didn't mean to push and I'm not a nosy, interfering matchmaker." At Maggie's lifted brow, Abby laughed. "Okay, at least I'm not most of the time, and I promise I won't be from now on. I just wanted to…" She shrugged.

"Check me out?"

Abby laughed. "Okay, that'll do."

Belle hollered again and Abby gathered her coat. "I'll see you later." She let herself out and Maggie went to get Belle.

The baby grinned when she saw her mother, and Maggie felt love swell inside her just as it did every time Belle turned that smile on her.

"Come on, kiddo. Let's go play until supper time." She checked to make sure Abby had locked the door behind her, then, for the next hour, Maggie entertained her daughter.

But Maggie couldn't quite keep focused on the playtime as her mind kept going back to the attempted robbery, the ugly sneer in the robber's voice as he demanded that she and Belle go with him. The dead squirrel with the nerve-shattering message that she was next.

Fear rumbled through her, and she swallowed hard.

Glancing through the French doors, she watched the sun dip lower in the sky. Soon it would be hidden, darkness would take over, and she wondered if tonight would be the night that the robber would make good on his threat and be back to kill her and Belle.

"Hey, we got a hit on the vehicle used in the robbery."

Eli's voice came over the phone and Reese set the weight he'd been curling with his left arm on the floor.

"Who does it belong to?"

"A guy by the name of Glenn Compton."

Reese wiped the sweat from his brow and blew out a breath. "You track him down yet?"

"Not yet. I'm in contact with the Bryson City P.D. and the Asheville P.D. I've got a Be On the Lookout order out on him, so hopefully we'll hear something soon. I'll send his picture to your phone."

His phone beeped, and he pulled it from his ear to check it. A text from Maggie that read, I'm Fine.

He smiled and pressed the phone back against his ear. "Okay, Maggie just texted, checking in, and said she was fine. All is okay for now."

"Glad to hear it. Let's do our best to keep it that way."

"You know it. In fact, I'm going to go over and check on things in about an hour."

"Because you think you need to or because it's a good reason to see a pretty lady?"

Reese smiled at the smirk in his friend's voice. "I think we both know the answer to that one."

Eli turned serious again. "I think that's a good thing, Reese. Holly and I've liked Maggie from the moment we met her. She's a special lady."

"I agree."

Back to business, Eli said, "Cal will be back in the office tomorrow. We'll add him to the protection rotation. He'll want to help."

"Good." Satisfaction and relief surged through Reese. The more people Maggie had watching over her, the better off she would be. "Keep me posted, Eli."

"You know I will."

Reese hung up and within seconds his phone buzzed. Eli had sent him Compton's picture. Bushy brows, ruddy complexion and a hard blue-eyed stare. Reese made note of the features, tucked his phone back in his pocket and stared at the wall. He'd been doing a little research on the man they had in custody before deciding to get in his daily exercise routine. He usually did his best thinking while working out. This time was no different.

Two of John Berkley's known associates were missing. Compton and a man named Douglas Patterson. Reese had examined the picture of Patterson and couldn't tell for sure if it was Slim, the man he'd shot, or not.

"Could be, though," he muttered.

He'd gone on to read that the three of them had been busted for a robbery in a small town just outside of Asheville. But they'd gotten off on a technicality—and the unwillingness of the only witness to come forward and testify.

In fact, that witness was now missing and presumed dead.

Reese rubbed his chin. Interesting.

If they had intimidated that witness to the point of sending him running, Reese felt sure that was their plan now with Maggie. Although, he frowned, he was also a witness and so far, everything had been directed at Maggie.

Was he next?

Or the tellers? No incidents with them had been reported, but that didn't mean something wasn't going to happen.

He made a mental note to ask Eli about keeping an eye on the tellers. He'd call and warn them to report anything suspicious. He'd also make an effort to stay extra alert.

The last thing he needed was to drop his guard and find himself with a bullet in his back.

Shaking off that thought, he glanced at his watch. Almost 5:30 p.m. He grabbed the bag that held Maggie's motion sensors and decided to make one more stop before heading her way.

Another knock on her front door didn't have the same effect on her heart rate as the earlier one. But she was still cautious as she placed Belle in her playpen and walked over to look out the window.

Reese was back. She couldn't help but think about Abby's comment that he was ready to move on.

But was Maggie? That was a question she didn't have an answer for right now. And didn't need to have one. She had time to get to know him and let him get to know her. And Belle.

She opened the door and he held up two bags from Holly Brody's Candy Caper shop and deli. "You were kind enough to feed me lunch, I thought I'd bring supper."

"Hmm…thank you. But…you really came to check on me, didn't you?" She smiled, not upset by that at all. She liked his company. She liked *him*. And she liked that he cared that she was safe. She felt as if she'd known him much longer than two days.

"Guilty as charged."

"Come on in."

He stepped inside and handed Maggie the bags of food and the motion sensors, then he shrugged out of his heavy coat, mimicking Abby's earlier actions. He hung the coat on the hook and moved into the kitchen while she placed the bags on the counter.

"I see you had company," he said. She lifted a brow at him and he grinned. "My awesome powers of observation. Two mugs in the sink."

Maggie smiled. "Abby came by."

He nodded. "She said she wanted to get to know you better. I'm glad she's making the effort to do so."

"It was nice having company. Gets kind of lonely around here with just Belle and me." She winced and prayed she didn't sound as desperate as she thought she did.

Reese gave a small, sad smile. "I know what you mean." Then shook off the melancholy her words seemed to bring on. Had she reminded him of his wife? Probably. "So let's eat. I'm starved."

"I'll get Belle."

Three hours later, Belle was asleep, and Reese was gone. Maggie smiled to herself as she thought about the evening. It had been nice. Pleasant.

Interesting.

She'd been able to forget everything that had happened over the past couple of days until Reese said, "I've got the alarm company scheduled to come first thing in the morning. I hope that's all right. He's a friend of Eli's and is fitting you into his busy day."

And she came back to earth with a thud. "It's fine."

Reality wasn't as pleasant as dinner with a handsome

man, but she agreed that the alarm system was necessary. And she needed it fast.

Maggie glanced out the window to see the cruiser sitting in his usual spot. Who was it tonight? Mitchell or one of the other deputies? She couldn't tell because of the darkness and the tinted windows. But satisfaction and thankfulness filled her because she knew if anyone got close to the house, the lights would come on.

Eli had mentioned having a bit of turnover lately, but she couldn't remember the names he mentioned. Not that it really mattered. There was only one deputy she was interested in, and she wasn't likely to forget his name anytime soon.

As she prepared for bed, she checked her phone. One message. From her sister-in-law, Shannon. So the woman was serious about visiting. Maggie wondered how she'd found her, as she hadn't told Shannon or anyone else where she was headed. She'd even used some of the techniques her police officer friend had told her about to cover her tracks for a while. Even though Kent had been dead, Maggie supposed she'd still been scared enough to feel as if she needed to become invisible. Being anonymous had been important to her the last few months.

She'd needed time to heal, to figure out what she wanted out of life. To find out who she was underneath Kent's robot. She supposed when she'd applied for a credit card last month, it probably hadn't been too hard to track her down.

Making a mental note to call Shannon tomorrow, Maggie checked on Belle one more time before slipping between the covers. She sent one last text to Reese, letting him know she was safe and was going to bed.

Then she lay there, eyes closed, thinking. Her mind turned one way then twisted another. *Go to sleep.*

The order did no good. Her eyes popped open. She forced them shut. After two hours of this, Maggie was ready to give up, get up and do some work, when a sound from the hallway startled her into sitting straight up in the middle of the bed.

Heart thumping, she peered out of her open door. What had she heard? Not moving, she just listened. Heard the sound of her own breathing. Maggie swung her feet to the floor. The blanket slipped from her shoulders and she pushed it to the side. Rising from the bed, she padded on silent feet into the hall. Belle's door stood open the way Maggie left it every night. The nightlight glowed, casting shadows Maggie used to think were comforting. Now they taunted her, their eeriness causing the hair on the back of her neck to rise and goose bumps to pebble up and down her arms.

Shivering, she walked into the den and crossed to the front door.

She checked the knob.

Locked.

Her blood slowed its frantic race through her veins. Maybe she'd fallen asleep after all and had been dreaming.

She walked into the kitchen, her bare feet soundless on the cold hardwood floors. Taking a deep breath, she flipped on the light.

And let the breath out slowly. All looked like she'd left it before heading to her bedroom earlier. A quick glance at the clock on the microwave said it was a little after 1:00 a.m. She turned the light off and blinked until her eyes adjusted again. Turning, she stepped and nearly screamed. Something soft—and squishy—slid between her toes.

Only the thought of waking Belle kept the scream from erupting from her throat. Gasping, she slapped the light switch once again and looked down.

A dark brown substance stained the floor next to her foot. "What—?" she whispered. Her stomach turned and she grimaced.

Kneeling, she touched the brown goo, lifted her finger to her nose and sniffed.

Dirt.

Relief threaded through her. Not blood or anything else along those lines. Just dirt. She could handle dirt.

Then she stiffened. But how had it gotten here? Had Reese tracked it in? But no. It hadn't been there when she'd gone to bed.

Her gaze flew to the kitchen door that led out to the small porch that overlooked the backyard. Now she noticed the dark round spots on the dark floor. Small round wet drops and traces of mud led from the door.

Her heartbeats came faster. How? Who? She'd locked the door. Double-checked it even after Reese had given the knob a test from the outside.

She heard something coming from her office and froze, her breath hitching in her throat.

Was someone in her house?

Belle.

Maggie raced down the hallway and into the baby's room.

The empty crib mocked her.

SEVEN

Reese rolled over and punched his pillow. He'd just checked with Jason White, the deputy assigned to guard Maggie's house tonight. Everything was fine. Quiet. She'd had her lights off now for a couple of hours.

It all sounded good. Maybe the robbers had decided to give it up. To stop hounding Maggie.

Right. He wished he believed that.

It would be nice, but he didn't live in a fantasy world. Reality was that Maggie was a target and until they caught everyone behind the attempted robbery, she would remain a target.

So the simple solution would be to find the other robbers. Hopefully, they'd hear something tomorrow. Reese glanced at the clock, sighed and rose. He walked to the window and pushed back the curtain just enough to look out across the lake. Maggie's place was lit up like a Christmas tree once again. He could make out the cruiser at the end of the gravel drive.

Reese couldn't say he was entirely comfortable with the placement of the cruiser. Where Jason sat, he could only see one side of the house. But when the man was making rounds, he walked the perimeter at least once an hour, staggering his timing so as not to have a pattern anyone could count on.

Reese rubbed his eyes and turned to head back to bed when a flash of red then blue flickering through the trees caught his attention.

"What's going on?" he whispered aloud. He waited, watching to see where the lights were headed.

Realized they were cruisers.

Cruisers heading toward Maggie's.

His gut clenched. Something had happened.

Bolting back to his room, he snagged his sweats and threw them on. Then he grabbed his gun and raced for his back door.

The sound of shattering glass brought him up short, and he turned to see a small round object on his bedroom floor. Reese's only thought was to make it out of the house before the bomb in his bedroom exploded.

Maggie felt her knees buckle. "Belle!"

Gathering her strength, she turned and raced to the front door and threw it open. The cruiser still sat at the end of her drive. "My baby's missing!"

At her frantic cry, Deputy Jason White opened the door and stepped out. The motion sensors blazed on. "What?"

Maggie felt tears slip down her cheeks. "Belle, she's not in her crib, she's...gone." The last word ripped from her throat and she thought she might throw up.

Before she could race back into the house, a loud crack ripped through the night air. Maggie spun around to see a bright flash light up the night sky. Across the lake.

Right where Reese's house was.

Reese's house?

She gaped then darted back into her house, desperate

to find Belle. *Please, let Reese be all right. And please, please let me find my baby.*

Sobs threatened to rip from her throat, but she couldn't afford the luxury of a good cry right now.

She went straight to the empty crib and gripped it with both hands as though touching it would allow her to touch Belle.

Deputy White stood behind her, speaking into his radio.

A high cry sounded. She froze as hope flooded her. "Belle?" she whispered as she ran toward the sound. The deputy again followed, his footsteps pounding right behind her.

Maggie rounded the corner of the door and raced into her office. She came to skidding halt on the hardwood floor. She blinked to make sure she wasn't seeing things. Belle stood in the playpen, holding on to the side, bottom lip quivering. Maggie rushed to her and snatched her against her. "Isabella, oh baby, you scared me to death."

"Is she all right?"

"Yes." Maggie inspected the little girl, running her hands over her head, her ears, her lips, her little fingers. "Yes, she's fine."

With the blinds drawn, flashing blue and red lights lit up the room as she carried Belle into the den. The deputy who'd been with her up to this point opened the door and let Eli Brody and Cal McIvers in.

"Maggie?" Eli asked. "What's going on?"

"What happened?" Reese demanded as he stepped inside behind Eli and Cal. "I heard the sirens then saw all the commotion over here and got here as fast as I could."

Maggie nearly lost it when she spotted Reese. "Your house?"

"Someone tossed an explosive in my bedroom as I was racing out. Fortunately, I got out before it went off." He glanced at Eli and Cal. "Fire trucks are on the way. We'll deal with that after we deal with this."

He'd left his own burning home to get to her, to make sure she was all right. The wild worry in his eyes conveyed a lot to her at that moment. She held herself together, clung to Belle and said, "Someone was in here. Someone moved Belle from her crib to the playpen in my office."

Eli and Cal exchanged a look. Deputy White nodded. Reese frowned. "Tell us what happened."

"I was trying to sleep," Maggie said, "and not being very successful at it when I heard a faint noise in the hall. I got up to check it and I came into the kitchen where I stepped in mud."

"Mud?" Cal lifted a brow.

"Yes. On the kitchen floor. Someone tracked it in." Reese went into the kitchen and the others followed. Maggie pointed to the floor. "See? It leads from this back door."

"Where does it go?" Eli asked.

Maggie shook her head. "I don't know. When Belle wasn't in her crib, I lost it."

"But she was in the playpen," Reese said. "Odd."

"Are you sure you didn't leave her in there and just thought you put her in the crib?" Deputy White asked.

Maggie stared at the deputy who'd been sitting in the cruiser outside her house while someone had been inside. "No, Deputy White. I didn't misplace my daughter. Someone moved her." The thought made her sick and she placed a kiss on top of the baby's head. Belle clapped her hands together and laughed, unaffected by the interruption of her sleep or the excitement going on around her.

Eli nodded then grimaced as he looked around. "Now that we've tracked all over it, let's make this an official crime scene. An attempted kidnapping. I'll get the kit. Maggie, I need you to take Belle back into the den and stay put while we see what we can do out here." He looked out the window toward Reese's home. "You'd better head back over there."

"I'll take care of that soon enough." He didn't look worried, but Maggie felt horrible that he was here with her when he was losing his home. His eyes softened as he looked at her, as though he knew what was going on inside her. "Go. It's all right. I didn't have anything too valuable anyway."

Maggie swallowed hard. She carried Belle into the den as ordered, but didn't sit. She hovered in the background to watch and listen. Because now she wasn't just scared...

...she was mad.

Reese slipped the mud from the kitchen floor into the evidence bag and ran his fingers across the top, sealing it. His thumping heartbeat had slowed considerably once he realized Maggie and Belle were safe, but his reaction to the flashing lights and sirens headed toward Maggie's house floored him.

He'd been terrified, more so than the moment he'd realized what was on the bedroom floor. His all-consuming fear of something happening to Maggie and Belle had nearly paralyzed him.

Reese looked at the deputy who'd been charged with keeping watch and wondered what the man had been doing while someone had been breaking into Maggie's house.

Anger rolled through him and he took a deep breath, pushing back the desire to lash out at the deputy and demand to know if he'd been sleeping on the job. Instead, he ran a hand through his hair and said, "Dust the doorknob for prints, would you?"

"Sure."

Reese followed the trail of dirt with his eyes then with his feet as it took him out of the kitchen, into the small foyer area and down the hall. A drop here, a drop there. The trail led straight into Belle's room. He was surprised Maggie hadn't stepped on either a water droplet or some of the mud before she'd found it in the kitchen.

Eli came up behind him. "Cal checked the door to the kitchen. No forced entry."

"Someone knows how to pick a lock?"

Eli shrugged. "Possibly. Or Maggie left it unlocked."

Reese was shaking his head before Eli finished the statement. "She's too careful about that. There's no way she left the door unlocked."

"The motion sensors didn't come on until Deputy White got out of his car," Maggie said.

"That means he didn't come through the front door. What about the door off the kitchen? That's where he gained access to the house."

Jason said, "I'll check."

Reese continued to follow the trail of mud, although it was faint now and he found fewer signs of the dirt as he went along to her office. But there beside the playpen was a trace of it. He could hear Belle starting to fuss and wanted to join her.

He looked inside the playpen and his eyes landed on a piece of paper. Snapping on the pair of gloves Eli handed him, he reached in and snagged the paper by the edge. He read aloud, "I could have taken her. Keep your mouth shut or you'll die like him."

He heard a quick, indrawn breath from behind him and turned to see Maggie standing in the hall, Belle on her hip. The baby rubbed her eyes and let out a wail. Maggie absently shushed her and asked, "What?"

Her pale face and trembling lips had him striding toward her. He handed the paper to Cal who bagged it. "Come back in here." Reese led her back into the den where she collapsed onto the couch.

Deputy White poked his head in the door. "The light over the kitchen door is broken." He shook his head. "I never heard it. I was doing my perimeter check like I was supposed to, I promise." He frowned, his face pale. "I...I'm sorry."

Reese just shot him a dark look. He left the others to finish the evidence gathering and reached out to take a squirming, whining Belle. Shock crossed Maggie's face, but she let him take the baby. He settled her on his lap and she looked up at him with those big brown eyes, her fussiness forgotten for a moment.

He swallowed hard and focused on Maggie. "Whoever broke in had no intention of taking Belle. He wrote that note before he got inside."

Eli ran a hand down his face and agreed. "He came here first, left the note, then went straight to Reese's house. He didn't want to take a chance on the explosion waking you up before he got in here and left his little message."

Maggie swallowed hard. "So what does this mean?"

"He's afraid you'll testify."

"But he's not even in custody," she sputtered.

"But his partner is," Eli reminded her.

"But die like...who?" she asked.

Reese drew in a deep breath and looked in the direction of his home. "Me."

Maggie didn't sleep much that night after everyone left. Instead, she worried. She knew she shouldn't, but she did. Cal McIvers sat outside her home the rest of the night, and she worried about him being too tired to stay awake. She worried about Reese and his damaged house, and she worried about keeping Belle and herself safe.

She walked into her office and saw the envelope on her desk. The one she'd meant to mail, but had forgotten in the chaos of worrying about everything.

Maggie was tired of worrying.

"Be anxious for nothing," she whispered aloud. Then with more conviction. "Be anxious for nothing, but in everything by prayer and supplication, with thanksgiving, let your requests be made known to God and the peace of God, which surpasses all understanding, will guard your hearts and minds through Christ Jesus."

She needed that peace that surpasses all understanding. Peace. Something she'd been searching for all her life, it seemed. Something she found only when she prayed and focused on God.

Please give me that peace, God.

He could give it to her, she believed that. Just as she'd believed He'd somehow take care of her and Belle when she'd been at her lowest point.

And He had. In a way she never would have guessed.

He'd used her grandfather. The grandfather she hadn't seen or heard from in over fifteen years.

The one who'd left her this modest lake house and a good chunk of money to put in her checking account along with a sizable trust fund for Belle.

Surprisingly, the money hadn't brought her peace. Yes, it had been a huge relief, but the peace had come in knowing God cared about her. He'd provided.

The knock at her door jerked her from her thoughts— and prayers. Maggie looked over at Belle who was jabbering and playing with her pacifier. Soon the baby's happy chatter would escalate to demands to be fed. Maggie scooped her up and settled her on her hip. Belle laughed and Maggie couldn't help but smile. *Thank you for this child, God.*

She carried Belle to the front door and peeked out the window. The cruiser still sat at the end of her driveway. Reese's truck had pulled in next to hers, and now he was standing on her porch.

And she looked like a frump. Old sweats and her hair in a ponytail. She hadn't even brushed her teeth yet. She grabbed a peppermint from the candy dish on the mantel and popped it in her mouth. The sweet candy tingled on her tongue, and she took a deep breath.

Maggie opened the door and waited for her heart to do that swooping thing it did whenever Reese smiled at her. The way he was doing now. "How are you this morning?"

"Tired and grumpy and worried." She matched his smile, though. "But at least we're alive, Belle's safe and I still have a house. How's yours?"

He shrugged. "The insurance adjuster will be out some-time today. The crime scene unit that came from Asheville called me this morning. The tech said the bomb wasn't very well put together. Sloppy, homemade and possibly deadly, depending on my location and what debris hit me. If I'd been in the room when it went off, it most likely would have killed me or done some pretty bad bodily damage, but the destruction is mostly limited to the bedroom and part of the kitchen, so the house isn't a total loss."

Maggie shivered and moved so he could come in. Reese stepped inside, making the small foyer seem even smaller. "But it does tell us one thing."

"What's that?"

"Whoever is after you—and now me—is serious. He doesn't mind killing." He reached out and touched her cheek. "Which means you've got to be extra careful."

Maggie swallowed hard. Not just at his words, but at the

trail of heat that followed his finger down her cheek. She wasn't sure what to think about her reaction to this man. "What about you?"

"I'll be careful, too."

Belle jabbered at him and after a moment of hesitation, he reached out and tapped her nose. "How are you this morning, Belle? Did you let your mama get some sleep after all the excitement?"

Belle ducked her head into Maggie's shoulder, and Maggie let happiness push aside the fear for a moment. Maybe he could learn to love Belle as well as…

She put a halt to those thoughts as she carried Belle into the kitchen. "She did. We both slept pretty well, considering everything that happened last night." She shook her head. "I moved her into my room, though. The terror I felt when I first saw she wasn't in her crib is still there."

"It may take a while for it to go away."

Maggie bent her head as Belle's bottle warmed on the stove. "I'll never forget that feeling," she whispered. "It's the same feeling I had once before, and I…" She trailed off and shuddered as she remembered the time she'd turned around in the grocery store for a bare minute. By the time she'd turned back, Belle and her stroller were gone. She'd found her the next aisle over, safe and sound with Shannon, her sister-in-law, hovering over her, but the feeling had been horrifying.

Another tremor rippled through her.

Reese's hands settled on her shoulder and she closed her eyes, relishing the comfort. Then Belle squirmed in her arms and reached for the bottle. Reese's hands fell away as Maggie juggled the baby and tested the milk on her wrist. She handed the bottle to Belle who promptly stuck it in her mouth.

"Let's go in the den so we can sit down."

He followed her and settled on the love seat while she took the recliner. Belle nestled in the crook of her arm, Maggie slowly rocked while the baby ate. He said, "Eli called me about an hour ago and said they got some footage off the bank's video cameras. It's not great, but he's hoping to get a response so he's circulating a picture of the robber I shot. His name may be Douglas Patterson, otherwise known as Slim. He's been known to hang out with Berkley and Compton. It looks kind of like him, but I couldn't say it's him for sure. Eli's also checked all the hospitals within a two-hour radius of us, but no one recognized Compton or the wounded man."

"He didn't get help, get his wound taken care of?"

"Probably not. The crime scene unit found the bullet in the wall by the door. It went straight through. I'm guessing Compton played doctor and patched him up."

Maggie shuddered.

Reese said, "We may even have a positive ID on the guy. Eli's checking it out."

"Who recognized him?"

"A gas station clerk in Asheville saw the newscast early this morning showing Compton's face and the picture from the bank camera. He called it in about three this morning."

Maggie felt a seed of hope sprout. "Maybe they'll catch them and this will all be over soon."

"I hope so." Reese was silent for a moment as he watched Belle eat. The creases in his forehead said he was thinking about something pretty deeply.

"What is it?" she asked.

"I was just wondering about you. We've spent quite a bit of time together, but I don't know a whole lot about you."

She lifted a brow at him. "I could say the same about you."

A flush appeared on his cheeks and she bit her lip on a smile. He nodded. "True enough."

Maggie studied him then said, "What do you want to know?"

"How did you come to live here? Where's your family?" He swallowed. "And if you don't mind my asking—what happened to your marriage?"

Maggie blew out a sigh. "You don't pull any punches, do you?"

Reese winced. "Sorry if that's too direct. I just… I want to know you."

And she wanted to know him, too. "My family is all gone. First my mother, then my grandmother. I never knew my father—he left when I was two."

"I'm sorry."

She shrugged. "I never missed him. My grandfather was there for the first eleven years of my life. He was my father figure."

"And he died, too?"

"No, he disappeared."

Reese lifted a brow. "Where'd he go?"

"I didn't know it at the time, but he came here. He left my grandmother for another woman."

"Ouch. That had to be awful for you all."

She nodded and ran a hand down her thigh. "It was. My grandmother was very angry, even bitter for a while, but then as the years passed, she gave it to the Lord and let Him heal her. I've never forgotten that."

"What about Belle's father's family?"

Maggie snorted and pursed her lips. "Kent's parents didn't like me and didn't want anything to do with Belle. He married beneath him, you see." Reese grimaced. Then her face softened. "But his sister, Shannon, was pretty good to me. And Belle. Especially Belle. She loved and accepted her from the moment she was born." Shame filled her. "When I left, I never told Shannon where I was going. I was so filled with hurt, anger, uncertainty. I just wanted to leave it all behind and start over. Start fresh." She paused. "I probably should have told her what I was doing." Maggie sighed. "But I didn't. I didn't want to talk to anyone, to see anyone, to explain anything to anyone. I just wanted to be alone."

"Any brothers or sisters?"

"No. I was an only child of only children. As I said, my father left when I was two. My mom told me he'd been killed in car wreck when I was about six, I believe. My mother died of a rare heart disease just after my twenty-second birthday and my grandmother died in her sleep shortly before I met Kent four years ago."

"I'm so sorry."

So she'd been lonely and still reeling from all the tragedies in her life. Easy pickings for the wrong kind of guy.

Maggie pulled the empty bottle from Belle's hands and placed the baby on the floor. Maggie handed her a toy that made a quiet noise every time Belle shook it.

Then Maggie began to pace. Belle looked up and watched for a moment, then went back to the book she now had clasped in both hands. She shook it and laughed as she shoved a corner into her mouth.

Maggie said, "Long story short, I was an abused wife. By the time I woke up and realized what I was allowing Kent to do to me, I had no real friends left. I was spending most of my time alone in my house, becoming a shell of the person I used to be. When I found out I was pregnant with Belle, Kent reacted horribly. He ordered me to get an abortion. I refused. For the first time since I'd known him, I stood up to him." Just remembering that feeling brought a smile to her lips. "It felt good. He threatened to cause me to have a miscarriage. I went to Shannon, and she was outraged at her brother's behavior—and thrilled that she was going to be an aunt. She let me stay with her."

"So you left him."

"Briefly. Kent found me there and started hitting me. Shannon called the police and he left. I told Shannon I couldn't stay there any longer. She begged me not to leave, but I couldn't put her in danger. I had a friend who was a police officer. Practically the one friend I had left from the church I had attended before I married Kent. At her house I was able to finish the last two classes I needed for my degree to teach. And Kent knew better than to harass me while I was with Felicia." A frown puckered her brow. "At least I thought he did. But a few months later, Kent came knocking on my door, begging me to come back, wanting to prove he was a changed man. Shannon came with him and vouched for him." Tears flooded her eyes. "He promised he was once again the person I'd dated and fallen in love with. I wanted to believe him," she whispered.

"But he hadn't changed."

"No." She cleared her throat and frowned. "Well, yes, he seemed to. He never laid a hand on me the rest of my pregnancy and we got along pretty well. But two days after Belle was born, the abuse started again. I knew then I had to leave for good or I was dead. And I couldn't leave Belle with him."

Reese felt his gut clench. How he wished Kent Bennett wasn't dead so he could plant a fist in the man's face and give him a taste of his own medicine. Reese unclenched his fist and forced his fingers to relax.

"So…" she paced to the small table next to the fireplace and looked at the pictures she'd arranged in a nice display "…there you have it."

"But you left and ended up here."

She sighed and settled back into the recliner. Belle crawled over and pulled herself up on her mother's knee. Maggie stroked the baby's head as she talked. "When Kent started hitting me shortly after we were married, I knew I'd messed up and that at some point I might need a safe place to go. The only person I could think of as a possibility for refuge, someone Kent didn't know about and couldn't threaten, was my grandfather. But I had no idea if he still cared about me."

"So you found him."

She shrugged. "It wasn't that hard."

"You contacted him?"

"No, not at first," she whispered. "I couldn't work up the courage. I walked around the house with his number in my pocket for weeks." She gave a watery laugh and blinked back tears.

Reese swallowed hard. "You don't have to talk about it if you don't want to."

"No, it's okay. It's part of who I am. I've moved past it, but I can't deny it." She pulled in a deep breath. "So then I found myself pregnant, abused and basically lost. At some point, I knew I was going to die if I didn't get out. I called my grandfather. He was thrilled to hear from me. Apparently, he'd been forbidden to have any contact with me after my grandparents' divorce and he went along with it. His new wife didn't want him involved with anyone from his old life and he agreed. She died the year I married Kent."

"So he wanted to see you?"

She nodded. "But I couldn't let him come to my house. I put him off, not daring to introduce him to Kent. Kent didn't like people in his house unless he'd invited them." She paused. "And I didn't want Kent to know about Grandpa."

"You were already planning to get away from Kent and go to your grandfather."

Maggie gave a slow nod. "But I had to be careful. If I moved too fast or left a trail, I knew he'd find me and kill me."

EIGHT

And he would have, too. She had no doubts about that.

Her phone rang, distracting her from her thoughts. Reese motioned for her to answer it. She glanced at the caller ID.

"Hello, Mrs. Adler."

"Hello, dear, how are you? I heard you had some excitement out there last night."

"We're fine. Have you recovered from finding that nasty little gift on my porch? I guess some teenagers are the same all over and like to have fun at other people's expense." She gave a small laugh that fell flat. Primarily because she didn't believe her own words. Most of the teens she worked with were great kids and would never do something like leave a dead squirrel on someone's doorstep with a threat attached. But Maggie tried to make light of the incident, not wanting the woman to be worried or scared.

"I don't know who would do a thing like that, but you definitely need to be careful, dear."

"I know." She glanced at Reese. "Deputy Kirkpatrick is working on helping me get a security system installed as soon as possible. In fact, the installers should be here soon."

A pause. "That's good." Another pause. "I, um… Well, the thing is, Maggie, ah…"

Suspicion hit Maggie. "Is there something you need to tell me?"

In a rush, the words came. "Oh, Maggie, Jim doesn't want me to come out to your house anymore because of everything that's happened. He's afraid I'll be involved and get hurt."

Maggie caught her breath. Then let it out slowly. "Oh."

"I'm so sorry. I tried to talk to him about it, but he was adamant and getting himself all worked up. I had to agree so he'd calm down. With his heart the way it is…"

"It's all right, Mrs. Adler. I really understand." Maggie didn't like it, but she did understand. "You have to take care of Mr. Adler."

"But what will you do with Belle while you're teaching?" she fretted.

"I…I'll figure something out. Your first priority is your husband. Once the police catch those bank robbers, all of this will stop and you can come back. I can make temporary arrangements for Belle."

"I'm just so sorry."

Maggie could tell the woman really was. Reassuring Mrs. Adler one more time that all would be okay, Maggie hung up, wondering what she was going to do about child care.

"You okay?"

Maggie picked Belle up and settled her into her lap. "Because of all that's happened, Mrs. Adler's not going to be able to take care of Belle while I teach anymore. I'm going to have to find someone else to watch her."

Reese frowned. "I'm sorry."

She gave a small shrug and frowned. "I'll figure something out."

"Are you still planning on going to the potluck dinner tonight?"

She bit her lip. "Should I?"

Reese didn't answer right away. Then he gave a slow nod. "I think it's all right. We'll be in public, and this guy's after you or me. No one else."

"But what if he does something that puts other people in danger?" She shook her head. "I don't think I should go."

Reese rubbed his chin and studied her. "No. You need to go. I want to watch the people there. I want to see how people interact with you."

She lifted a brow. "You mean use me as bait?"

"No, absolutely not. I just want to observe those you interact with. I'm not trying to catch anyone tonight." He paused. "And if I think there's even a hint of danger, I'll get you out of there faster than you can blink, all right?"

Maggie gave a slow nod. "All right."

The knock on her door pulled Reese to his feet. "Your alarm installers are here."

After the alarm system was installed, the afternoon passed in a blur of teaching and taking care of Belle. Finally, it was five o'clock and Reese would be there in fifteen minutes to take her and Belle to the potluck dinner. At the thought, her stomach rumbled in anticipation. But her nerves trembled.

Was she making a mistake? Should she stay home? But what was she going to do? Stay inside the rest of her life? Constantly worry that the bank robber would show up and make good on his threat?

Maybe.

Anger swelled inside her. Why did it seem as if the people who tried to do the right thing always got knocked down while those who did everything they weren't supposed to do got off scot-free?

It wasn't fair.

Then again, nothing had been *fair* since she'd met and married Kent. And, truly, it wasn't about fairness. It was about living her life the way she'd determined to live it the day she'd decided to get away from the abuse.

She hadn't run from her marriage. In fact, she'd never planned to marry again as long as Kent was alive. But she wasn't going to be his punching bag, either.

Maggie lifted her chin as she thought about the dead squirrel and the nasty threat. Well, if she was *next* as the note said, she wasn't going down without a fight.

Maggie gathered Belle's bag of baby essentials and her purse and set them on the floor beside the door. Belle played in her playpen, happy to clean it out by throwing the toys on the floor. Then she'd yell and Maggie would fill it up again. Only to begin the game all over again.

But Maggie didn't mind. Belle was happy, and that was all that mattered.

When Reese's knock came, she was ready. She opened the door and swallowed hard. He had on jeans, a pullover sweater with his heavy coat thrown over it, but not zipped.

And he looked good.

Ignoring her heart's sudden increase in beats per minute, she smiled. "Right on time."

"I was ready to see you." His bluntness made her blink but his grin set her at ease.

"Well...thanks."

He laughed and bent to pick up her purse and baby bag. "I'll carry them to the truck while you get Belle."

She handed him the items. "I'll drive if you don't mind. I've already put the beans in the back of my truck. I don't want to have to transfer her car seat base to your truck and then back to mine. It's just easier to drive."

Reese nodded and walked to her truck. She unlocked it with the remote then went to get Belle.

The baby grinned up at her and Maggie felt love consume her. She picked up Belle and set her on her hip, saying a prayer of thanksgiving to God for blessing her with the child. Then she went to meet Reese.

In the car, she drove automatically while she noticed Reese watching the mirrors. "Are you sure this is a good idea?" she asked, her fingers tightening around the steering wheel as her stress level increased at the thought of being followed to the church.

He didn't take his eyes from the rearview mirror. "I think you'll be fine, Maggie. This guy has shown himself to be sneaky, preferring to leave things on your porch or try to get to you in the middle of the night. I really don't think we have anything to worry about at a church full of people." He reached over and covered her tense, cold fingers with his warm hand. "And don't forget, the entire Rose Mountain police force will be there. On duty and ready for trouble if it happens."

That did make her feel a bit better. "All right." She forced a smile. "Then let's go have a good time."

Reese wasn't quite as sure about the man who'd threatened Maggie as he'd led her to believe. Not that he doubted his reassurances, but he was making his judgments based on experience. Everything he'd told her was true. He just hoped this time didn't turn out to be the exception to the rule.

No, there was no hoping for that. He firmed his jaw. He'd make sure of that. He'd stick with Maggie and Belle like superglue to ensure they were safe and had a good time. In the meantime, he'd do his best to put her at ease. She needed to relax. But…he looked at her and said, "I meant what I said about believing you'll be safe, but…"

"But what?"

"But don't go anywhere alone. Even to the restroom, okay?"

Worry wrinkled her forehead once again and Reese grimaced. But as much as he wanted her to enjoy herself, she had to keep her guard up. Her lips flattened but she gave a short nod.

When Maggie pulled into the parking lot, Reese was surprised at the number of people there. "This must be a popular activity for the church."

Maggie nodded. "Holly said it's an annual tradition. The church supplies the turkey and everyone brings enough side dishes to serve a cruise ship."

Reese smiled at that picture. Maggie unbuckled her seat belt and climbed out to get Belle from the backseat. "But," she said, "the good thing about this is the church invites everyone in the community. They even have volunteers who deliver meals to people who can't get out to come eat. Which is why I brought that huge thing of green beans."

She set Belle's carrier on the ground beside her.

"Nice." He frowned. "I didn't realize that or I could have helped."

"I think you get a pass your first visit."

"This is your first dinner here and you didn't take a pass. You brought beans." She smiled at him and pulled the beans from the truck. His breath seemed to lodge somewhere between his chest and his throat as her eyes crinkled at the corners. She really was a beautiful woman. And a strong one, he thought, as, with beans in one hand, she lifted Belle's car carrier in the other. He quickly offered, "You want me to carry her?"

She lifted a brow at him. "Would you?"

"Sure."

"Then, thanks." She started toward the church and Reese glanced down at Belle, who looked like a miniature mummy wrapped in blankets. The small pink hat came down over her ears. Brown eyes studied him. He grasped the handle and lifted her. Carrying a baby in a carrier was different than carrying one in his arms. With his fingers wrapped around the handle, he didn't feel the sharp pang of grief and remembrance he did when he held a small body in his hands.

A small, fragile body, devoid of life—

He inhaled, his lungs protesting the sudden intake of frigid air. As he exhaled, he noticed Maggie almost to the door. She turned. "Are you all right?"

"Yeah." He forced a smile. "We're coming."

She waited until he caught up then held the door open. He let her pass in front of him and followed her inside.

Smells of home cooking tantalized him and his stomach rumbled. Home-cooked meals were few and far between unless he put forth the effort—which he rarely did. This was a real treat. He looked at the woman beside him and the baby carrier in his grip.

And swallowed hard at the picture the three of them made.

If the people in the small church didn't know the truth, they would probably think Reese, Maggie and Belle were a family.

The thought didn't bother him nearly as much as he thought it might. In fact, it just occurred to him that his first impulse had been to volunteer to carry Belle—not the beans.

He smiled and hope stirred. Maybe the big hole in his heart would one day heal after all.

Maggie set the green beans on the table with the other food. She unwound the scarf around her neck and shrugged out of her heavy coat. Pegs lined the wall near the door and she hung everything on one.

Reese stood beside her holding Belle, and she shivered at how they must look.

They could be a family.

Her stomach flipped at the idea and a small smile curved her lips. Then a niggling of doubt pressed in, causing her smile to droop. Memories of a bad first choice threatened to consume her. She refused to let it happen.

"Thanks for carrying her. She gets heavy."

"No problem." He set the carrier on the nearest table as people stopped by to speak to them. Holly and Eli were the first to greet them. Eli clapped Reese on the shoulder. "Glad you could make it."

Maggie released Belle from her safety restraints and smiled as Mrs. Adler started toward her, arms open, delight—and determination—in her eyes. "Jim may not want me to come over and watch her at your house anymore, but I can enjoy her here at the church all I want. I'll take her while you eat if you like. I'm not the least bit hungry right now."

"Nibbled a little too much when you were helping put the stuff out?" Maggie teased.

Mrs. Adler grinned. "You know it."

"Then, sure, I'd love for you to entertain Belle for a while. Thanks." Maggie watched the sweet woman take Belle over to another woman with a baby about the same age as Belle. She couldn't begrudge Mrs. Adler time with Belle just because her husband was worried about her being at the house where all the strange things were happening.

She knew Mrs. Adler loved Belle as if she were one of her own grandchildren.

Grief pierced her with a sudden jab. It should have been

her mother, Belle's natural grandmother, coddling and kissing her.

Reese's hand on her arm pulled her from her sad thoughts. "Are you all right? Something wrong?"

Maggie shook her head. "No. It's nothing. Nothing I can do anything about." She pulled in a deep breath and smiled at Holly. A pale and wan-looking Holly. "How are you feeling?"

"Sick." The woman grimaced then grinned as her eyes trailed after the teen who had volunteered to entertain her almost three-year-old son, Daniel.

Maggie felt her heart lighten. "I remember the feeling well."

"But I'm glad to be here where I can let someone else chase that rascal for a bit."

A pretty blond woman walked up and gave Holly a hug. She looked at Maggie and offered a friendly smile. "I'm Paige Seabrook."

"Dylan's wife. I've heard about you. Nice to finally meet you," Maggie said.

"I hear you're having some trouble since the bank robbery," Paige said, then grunted as a toddler hurled himself at her legs. She bent down and picked him up as a boy about ten years old came rushing up.

"I was chasing him. He's fast!"

Paige grinned. "Maggie, these are my two boys, Will and David."

Will held out a hand and Maggie shook it. He smiled. "Nice to meet you." Then he was gone, chasing after a buddy who'd tagged him, leaving David for Paige to wrestle with as he wanted to go with Will.

Paige shook her head, motioned to Dylan to watch the boy as she set him on his feet and watched him go. Dylan started off after him. "They grow so fast." Then her expression turned serious as she returned to the conversation they'd been having before the interruption. "Have you had any more incidents since yesterday?"

Maggie frowned. "No. I was worried about coming here, afraid my presence might put everyone in danger, but Reese said we'd be safer here than at home." She sighed and shook her head. "I really hate that they went after Reese, too."

Holly nodded. "Eli told me about the bomb in Reese's house." She gave a shudder. "How awful."

"I know. Now he's living out of his boathouse and checking up on me every hour or so." Maggie's gaze homed in on Reese and her heart flipped that crazy little cartwheel it liked to do whenever she looked at the man. He still stood with Eli and Dylan. Cal had joined them. "Where's Abby?"

Holly kept one eye on the teen carrying her son, Daniel, around. "She had a delivery at the hospital in Bryson City." Holly turned back to Maggie. "Eli's briefed me each night about the latest happenings, then given me descriptions of who to watch for and orders to keep my doors locked, don't answer the door if I don't know who's there, and so on." She said it with amusement, but the concern in her eyes was real.

Maggie shivered and looked around, wondering if her attacker had followed her to the potluck dinner. She bit her lip, praying she hadn't led trouble to the doorstep of these innocent people.

"Looks like Pastor Collins is getting ready to say the blessing," Holly murmured. As if on cue, the crowd quieted and Pastor Collins blessed the meal.

When he was done, everyone made a beeline for the food-laden tables. Maggie hung back, eyeing the crowd, wondering if the man who'd been terrorizing her was here.

Was he watching?

Waiting for a chance to strike?

Fear tightened her gut and her breath wanted to short out.

"You ready to get a plate?"

Reese's quiet voice settled her nerves immediately. She nodded, eyes on Belle's happy face. "That sounds good."

He led her to the line and she savored his presence beside her.

She just couldn't help feeling that someone was watching. And waiting.

Waiting for a chance to make his move.

"I'm going to get a high chair," Holly said from behind her. "Do you need one for Belle?"

"Yes, that would be great." She frowned. "I guess I could feed her in her carrier, but she likes a high chair better."

"I'll get them for you," Reese offered. "Where are they?"

"In the—"

"Sorry to interrupt. I need to speak to Reese for a minute. We may have a lead on the bank robbery." Eli motioned Reese to the side. Reese smiled an apology and followed Eli to a far corner where Cal waited, phone pressed to his ear.

Holly shrugged. "I can get them."

"I'll come with you," Maggie insisted. "You can't carry two high chairs at the same time."

"True. They're down the hall in the closet next to the bathrooms."

Maggie followed Holly from the fellowship hall into the corridor. As the door shut behind them, the loudness of so many people in one room was muted to a low buzz. Maggie laughed. "My ears are ringing."

Holly grinned then grimaced as she placed a hand over her stomach.

Concerned, Maggie touched the woman's shoulder. "Are you all right?"

"Just really queasy. I've eaten my weight in crackers and it helps, but…" She pulled in a deep breath and swallowed hard. "I'll be all right. Let's get those high chairs." She started down the dark hall. "There's a light switch around here somewhere. Try your side, I'll try this one."

Maggie felt along the wall and a few seconds later, her fingers found the switch. "Here it is."

She flipped it and light flooded them.

"That's better. It's spooky in here without any light." Holly gave a small laugh, but Maggie had to shake off an uncomfortable sudden fear of being separated from the rest of the group.

But she was with Holly. They'd be fine.

Her footsteps echoed as she followed Holly past the restrooms on the right then around the corner to a room labeled Kitchen Storage. "Here we are," Holly said as she pulled the key from the band around her wrist. She inserted it into the lock and opened the door. Reaching in, she flipped the light on.

Then turned with wide eyes and a distinctly green cast to her pretty face. "I'll be in the bathroom for a few minutes." She bolted back down the hall to the restroom, leaving Maggie standing in the storage room.

"Poor thing," Maggie whispered aloud. She'd been a little nauseous with Belle, but hadn't had Holly's problem. She looked around and spied a row of high chairs. They didn't look very heavy and she thought she might be able to carry both at the same time if she balanced them right.

Maybe.

When the hallway behind her went dark, Maggie froze.

NINE

"Holly?" Maybe she'd come back and hit the light switch by mistake. "Holly? Are you there?"

Silence.

Okay, it wasn't Holly. She would have answered. Maggie's stomach twisted. What should she do? Venture into the dark hall and look for the light switch? Or stay here and wait for Holly to come back from the restroom?

Then she remembered Reese's instructions. Don't go anywhere alone. Stay with someone, even when you go to the restroom.

Trembling started from deep within. Had he followed her here? To the church?

A resounding yes echoed inside her. It was him. The light going off wasn't an accident. And he could probably see her standing in the doorway of the lighted storage closet.

She slapped the switch and plunged them into darkness.

A light footfall fell to her right. From the direction of the restroom.

She moved further inside the small room.

But what about Holly? What if she came out of the restroom and the man attacked her?

Maggie stepped back out into the hall. The hair on the

back of her neck stood at full attention. Should she scream and bring everyone running?

Would anyone even hear her through the thick doors that separated the roar of the crowd from this hall?

No, no one would hear, except maybe Holly.

She knew it.

He knew it.

Maggie moved on silent feet down the hall, all sense tuned to the area around her. She prayed to feel any air shift, a hint of cologne or body odor, anything that would tell her he was near.

On trembling legs, she continued her slow tread to the restroom where Holly was. Her fingers trailed the wall even as her mind pictured the door. The first one she came to would be the bathroom.

Fingertips hit the doorjamb just as the bathroom door flew open.

Holly let out a surprised squeal as Maggie pushed her inside, slammed the door shut and locked it.

A heavy fist crashed against the thin wood and Maggie stared at a still-shocked Holly, knowing they didn't stand a chance if the attacker outside decided to kick it in.

"Hey," Reese asked Eli. "Where did Maggie and Holly go?"

Eli looked around and shifted Daniel from his shoulders to the floor. "I don't know. I've been so busy keeping up with this guy I didn't notice that she was missing." He gave a rueful smile then a sympathetic grimace. "She's probably in the bathroom being sick again."

Reese winced at the thought. "But where's Maggie?"

"Oh, she went to get a high chair for Belle. I think Holly went with her," Paige said. "When they came back, I was going to get one for David." She let her eyes scan the crowd. "But they're not back yet." A frown pulled her lips down. "And they should be. The closet is just outside in the hall."

Reese and Eli exchanged a glance. A bad feeling swept through Reese before he could stop it. He headed for the big double doors without another word. Eli was on his heels. He told himself he was just being paranoid, but that didn't stop his blood pressure from skyrocketing and his worry meter from jumping into high.

Pushing through the doors, he stepped into darkness. "Maggie?"

Running footsteps sounded. "Eli, where's the light?"

"Right here."

The hallway lit up. Empty.

Where were they?

A door slammed from the hall that branched to the right. Eli took off in that direction. "I'll check that out. You find Maggie and Holly!"

Reese placed a hand on his weapon and scanned the hallway once again. His eyes landed on the bathroom door just as his cell phone started ringing.

Maggie's tone.

He grabbed his phone from the clip on his belt. "Maggie, are you all right?"

"Someone's in the hallway. Holly and I are in the bathroom." Her terror-filled voice came through the line, singeing his brain and firing his fury at the person doing this to her.

"I'm right outside the door." No sooner had the words left his lips than the door flew open and Maggie's scared face stared up at him. Holly's wide eyes and pale cheeks sent his tension level soaring. "Go back into the crowd and stay there. Tell Cal what's going on and to listen to his radio. I'm going to go after Eli and see if I can help him find whoever was in the hall." Reese spoke into his radio. "I've got Maggie and Holly. They're fine. You catch the guy?"

"Not yet," Eli's disgusted response came back. "I'm at the back of the church. Check the front."

Reese's left hand curled into a fist and he had to make an effort to relax it as he watched as Holly and Maggie safely made it back through the double doors.

Then he spun on his heel and made his way to the side door that led outside. Darkness covered him. Silence made his ears ring.

He stood for a moment to let his eyes adjust. Then he opened them to scan the area. Nothing but the church parking lot. But lots of cars to hide behind.

Reese made his way down the steps, around the side of the building, his gun ready, senses alert. Eli's voice came over the earpiece he'd tucked into his left ear in order to keep the radio quiet. "Hey, any luck?"

"Nothing," he said, keeping his voice low. At the front of the church, he probed each and every shadow, the bushes, the cars on the curb. "He's gone."

"Or hiding, watching us chase our tails," Eli grunted.

"Yeah, I'm feeling a bit exposed. Let's get back inside and check on Maggie and Holly." Eli pulled his cell phone from his pocket. "Jason's on duty, but I noticed he's not here tonight. He said he was going to stop by and grab some food." Eli shook his head. "Guess he changed his mind. I'll get him over here to do a sweep with the big light."

Reese nodded. "I'll meet you back inside." He itched to make sure Maggie was all right. Within seconds, he was in the social hall and standing at the edge of the crowd, searching for her blond head.

Finally, he spotted her at a table in the back, Belle in her lap, spooning food into the little one's mouth. He made his way to her and noticed that Holly had Daniel seated on some hymnals. Holly shrugged as she noticed the direction of his glance. "I wasn't going back to get a high chair."

"Me, either." Maggie shuddered, her eyes troubled.

Reese didn't have any problem figuring out what it was that bothered her. "It's not your fault, Maggie."

"If I hadn't come, then none of this would have happened." She kept her voice low, but he caught the slight tremble that shook her words.

Reese rested a hand on her shoulder and squatted in front of her and Belle. He looked into her eyes and said, "You have every right to be here. Letting him scare you into taking precautions is smart. We did that tonight and you're fine. Letting him ruin your life is not going to happen. Not as long as I'm around. Got it?"

He saw her swallow then give a slow nod. "I agree, but I can't put other people in danger anymore, either. If something had happened to Holly tonight..." She bit her lip. "I can't do that anymore."

Reese glanced around, then sighed. "You may be right. He's escalating, becoming more bold. Trying to get to you in the middle of a crowd like this..." He shook his head. "I didn't think... I'm sorry. I really thought it would be fine for you to come. I'll stay right by your side for as long as you want to stay, then I'll take you home and make sure you're safely inside."

"Then what?"

"Then we keep our eyes open, watch our backs and catch him the minute he lifts his head."

For the next week, Maggie's nerves stayed wound up tight. At night, her adrenaline surged at the slightest sound. During the day, she kept the doors locked, the alarm on and only took Belle outside if the deputy on duty was by her side.

A lot of times that deputy was Reese.

In fact, it was more times than not, she'd noticed. As the days passed and she spent more and more hours in his presence, getting to know him and finding out the little things that made him tick, Maggie realized she could fall hard for this man.

If it wasn't for his reluctance to be around Belle. True, he'd held the baby the night someone had broken in, but she didn't think he'd really wanted to.

And that hurt.

Maggie sighed and logged off the computer. For the past few days, she'd juggled her classes and Belle, while trying to find child care. Fiona, Cal's sister, had volunteered to watch Belle today at their ranch while Maggie worked. It was Cal's day off, and he was there to keep an eye on everyone, including his nephew, one-year-old James. Abby was working late and Joseph, Fiona's husband, was on a horse-buying trip. Brother and sister would hold down the fort and take care of the two children.

Now that her classes were done for the day, the house echoed its silence. She missed Belle and her baby chatter, but Maggie had to admit that she was looking forward to enjoying the time to herself for the next two hours.

The phone rang and she jumped. Placing a hand over her racing heart, she wondered if she'd ever be able to fully relax again.

"Hello?"

"I hear you have some free time."

She smiled at Reese's statement. "How'd you hear that?"

"Cal told me. He offered extended babysitting services if you were to accept my invitation."

"Invitation?" The blood started to hum in her veins.

"I wondered if you might like to have dinner with me."

A date? Maggie felt her stomach start to twist itself in knots. *No* hovered on the tip of her tongue.

But she wanted to go.

The week had been slow and had seemed to drag on forever as she'd waited for something else to happen. Something bad. Nothing had happened and she still couldn't let go of the tension.

"Maggie?"

She'd been silent too long. "That sounds lovely, Reese. I'd love to, thanks."

A relieved sigh filtered through the line. "You had me worried there for a minute. How about five o'clock? We'll drive in to Bryson City."

"I'll be ready."

Maggie hung up and just sat there for a moment. It was a little past three o'clock. She had two hours. She wondered if it would be enough time to figure out what she was going to wear.

An hour and a half later, she was ready. Maybe.

Nervousness twisted inside her.

The knock on the door startled her. A quick glance at the clock said four-thirty. Was Reese early?

Hurrying to the door, she peered out the window.

And nearly fell over in shock.

Maggie twisted the knob and threw the door open. "Shannon?"

The pretty brunette smiled. "Hello, Maggie." The woman looked Maggie up and down and then nodded. "You're looking good. Widowhood seems to agree with you."

Maggie threw her guard up. "At least it doesn't leave bruises," she snapped.

"Very true. My brother was a rat. You're well rid of the

man. Now may I come in before the officer in your driveway decides to arrest me?"

Maggie stepped back and got a good whiff of Shannon's strong perfume as the woman whipped past her and into the den. Her jeans hugged her perfect figure, the aqua-blue blouse brought out the color of her eyes, and her makeup had been applied with an expert hand.

Shannon looked amazing. As always.

Maggie said, "I've had some…trouble. The officer is there to make sure a certain bank robber doesn't follow through on his threat."

"Bank robber?"

"It's a long story. I didn't know you'd be coming so soon. I thought you'd call or let me know when to expect you."

"I know. I'm sorry. I just managed to get away faster than I thought. I didn't want to waste any more time than necessary in getting here." She plopped on the couch. "Now, where's my Isabella? I can't wait to see her." The excitement in Shannon's eyes melted Maggie's ire with her high-handed ways and airs of superiority.

"She's not here."

Disappointment fell all over the woman. "Oh, well that's just not what I wanted to hear. Where is she?"

"With some friends. I have a…" What did she have? Did she dare call it a *date?* "I'm having dinner with a friend. He should be here soon."

"Dinner with a friend? A male friend?" Shannon let out a small laugh. "My dear, that's called a date."

Maggie resisted the urge to roll her eyes. But she couldn't help the small smile. "Maybe that's what you call it, but I'm simply calling it dinner. If it becomes more than two friends getting together for a meal…well, we'll just see how it all plays out before we put a label on it, okay?"

"Sure, whatever you say."

"Now, where are you staying?"

With a manicured fingernail, Shannon picked at nonexistent lint on her jeans. "I've got reservations at that quaint little B and B on Main Street, but I'm not sure how long I'll stay there. It's ridiculously expensive for a rinky-dink town like this."

Maggie's brow rose. Shannon worried about money? That was a new one. "Rose Mountain is a wonderful town, Shannon. If you'll give it a chance, I think you'll come to love it."

Shannon pursed her lips. "Hmm. Maybe." She sighed. "I suppose I don't have a choice. I sold my house."

Maggie gaped. "You what? Why would you do that?"

A delicate shrug lifted the woman's shoulder. "I was tired of it. I wanted to do something new."

"But what about your job?"

"I quit. It was boring."

Concerned, Maggie simply stared at Shannon. Would the woman never grow up? Granted, she didn't have to work, but from what Maggie remembered, she'd seemed to enjoy it. And this was the woman she was going to leave Belle with if something happened to her? She sighed. No, she needed to figure that out soon. Shannon's impromptu visit just reinforced that decision.

The doorbell chimed and Maggie rose. "That's probably Reese." She walked to the door and peeked out. In spite of herself, her heart picked up its pace and her palms went slick. Pulling in a steadying breath, she twisted the knob. "Hi."

He grinned down at her. "Hey, there. You look gorgeous."

"So do you." The words slipped out before she could stop

them and she felt a flush creep up the back of her neck. His grin widened and his eyes held a decidedly pleased look.

Maggie cleared her throat and stepped back, motioning him in. "There's someone here I want you to meet." Curiosity had him lifting a brow and stepping inside. "I wondered who the car outside belonged to."

She led him into the den and said, "Reese Kirkpatrick, meet my former sister-in-law, Shannon Bennett."

The two shook hands. Maggie thought Shannon allowed her grip to linger a bit longer than necessary and was surprised by the little dart of jealousy she felt. Shannon was a beautiful woman. Would Reese...

He turned to Maggie and she could see conflict on his face. Before he had a chance to say anything, Maggie said, "Shannon, you're welcome to stay here if you like."

"Oh, no. I'll just get checked in to my room at the B and B and see you later." She frowned and bit her lip, looking uncertain. A very un-Shannon-like look. "Will you call me tomorrow?"

"Sure. I have your number from when you called me last week."

"Okay, thanks. Y'all have fun." And then she was gone, leaving Maggie blinking at her sudden perfume-laden departure.

"Wow," Reese said.

"Exactly."

"I don't think Rose Mountain is prepared for her."

"I don't think it's possible to prepare for Shannon. I think all you can do is hang on and hope you don't get tossed off the life raft when the waves start crashing in."

Reese laughed, but Maggie wasn't so sure she meant her statement to be funny. She had enough chaos in her life right now. Adding Shannon into the mix was enough to twist her stomach in knots and set her nerves on edge.

* * *

Maggie hung up the phone after checking on Belle, and Reese wondered if she would stay deep in thought the whole night or just during the ride to Bryson City. "Anything you want to talk about?"

Maggie started. "Oh, sorry. Just thinking."

"About?"

She let out a sigh. "Everything." Then seemed to shake it off. "But tonight's supposed to be fun. I don't want to talk about worries and troubles. Belle is in good hands, and I'm going to dinner for the first time since she's been born without her on my hip. It feels good." She smiled at him and his heart lightened. He really liked this woman.

A lot.

But he wanted to tell her about his baby girl and how she'd died. He needed to explain why he was so uncomfortable around Belle. Although, he had to admit, he was getting better the more he was around her.

But Maggie said she didn't want to talk about worries and troubles. He reached over to grasp her hand. "Okay, I have one thing we need to talk about and then we can put all serious stuff aside and just focus on enjoying ourselves. You want to talk about it now or at the end of the da—er, dinner?"

She turned slightly in her seat to face him and squeezed his hand. "We can talk about anything you want."

"Okay." He pulled in a deep breath and prayed he could get the words out without tearing up. Clearing his throat, he said, "You know my wife died about eighteen months ago."

"Yes."

"Well, what I didn't tell you was that she died in childbirth."

A gasp whispered from her lips and her hand tightened even more around his. "Oh, Reese, I'm so sorry."

"She had an aneurysm. The baby, a little girl we'd named Emma, died, too." He cleared his throat again, hoping to dislodge the knot that always formed there when he talked or thought about his baby.

When Maggie didn't say anything, he looked over at her to see tears standing in her eyes. He quickly looked back at the road. Taking the longer route on the back roads to Bryson City had seemed like a good idea at the time. He'd gotten off I-74 and turned onto the Blue Ridge Parkway. His purpose had been to keep her in the car with him as long as possible in order to give him plenty of time to get the words out. Now they were out and he wished he'd taken the shorter route. At least in the restaurant, there wouldn't be the silence surrounding him.

He finally heard Maggie draw in a deep breath. "Well, that explains a lot."

"Like what?"

"Like why you're so reluctant to hold Belle and be around her."

"Oh. You noticed that, huh?"

She flashed him a watery smile. "It's kind of hard not to."

"I'm sorry, Maggie. Belle is a beautiful child. It's just hard sometimes because when I'm around babies, the memories seem to crash in with more force. The memories, the emotions, the…loss, it just all seems magnified."

"I'm sure."

He drove in silence for the next few miles then asked, "Have I ruined our evening by telling you this?"

For a moment, she didn't answer, then she gave his hand another squeeze and said, "No way. We both need this. I'm glad you told me." More silence, then, "So how's living in the boathouse working for you?"

He gave a surprised laugh at the change of subject. "It's

fine for the next couple of weeks until my house is put back together."

Reese caught sight of headlights coming up fast behind him. Keeping his eye on the rearview mirror, he sped up. The person following him jammed the gas, and before Reese could do the same. The impact slammed him forward against the seat belt.

TEN

Maggie screamed as the seat belt cut into her right shoulder and jerked her back against the seat. Reese's truck swerved to the right then back into the lane as he fought for control. "Get your phone and call Eli!"

Maggie bent and grabbed her purse from the floor, slipped her fingers into the side pocket and pulled out her phone. She didn't know if she'd be able to hear over the pounding of her heart and the squealing tires.

"Here he comes again," Reese warned, his voice tight, knuckles white on the wheel.

Maggie felt her muscles brace for the next impact and sent up a desperate prayer. Metal crunched metal as she kept a tight grip on the phone. She slammed forward then back, her elbow hitting the door. Pain raced up her arm and she ignored it as Reese jerked the car to the left, pressed the gas pedal and zoomed forward.

Her fingers found the touch pad of the phone and it lit up. "What's Eli's number?" she gasped.

He told her and she punched it in then held the phone to her ear. "No, call 911. Eli's too far away."

She hung up and hit the three digits that would bring help. She hoped. Her heart beat fast, adrenaline made her fingers tremble.

The car swerved left, then right. She didn't even want to know where they were on the mountain. She was almost glad for the dark. At least she couldn't see how far she had to fall if the car shot through the guardrail.

The phone rang. Then cut off. "No cell signal, Reese."

"That's why he waited until this moment to attack. I'm an idiot. I should have stuck with the highway."

A car whizzed by on the left and Reese muttered, "We've got to stop this guy or someone's going to get killed."

Trembling, she tried the phone again. "911. What's your emergency?"

"Someone's trying to run us off the road. We're on the Blue Ridge Parkway about…"

"A mile from Highway 19!" Reese hollered.

He swerved around the next bend then jerked the wheel to the left to hit the next curve. The car behind them closed the distance and Reese slammed on the brakes as he rounded the curve on two wheels. Maggie squelched a scream and simply held on as she prayed.

Sparks flew from the car behind them as it ran along the guardrail. It fell back a few feet and Reese raced to make the turn onto the highway.

"Look!" She gestured to the blue lights heading their way.

"Thank God."

Reese approached the intersection of Highway 19 and slowed. Maggie kept an eye on the car behind them. It raced up and Reese jerked to the left at the last minute into the oncoming-traffic lane.

Their attacker roared past and squealed around the corner onto Highway 19, barely missing an oncoming car. Horns blared and the Bryson City police cruiser took up the chase.

Reese braked to a stop on the side of the road. Maggie

leaned her head against the window and closed her eyes, offering a hearty thank-you prayer that they were still alive.

"That was scary." Reese's rumble filled the car.

"I can't believe you didn't go over the side."

"I was number one in my class when it came to defensive driving."

"That's good. You did good."

The inane conversation helped to calm her. Reese finally opened the door and flashed his badge at the approaching officers. Maggie climbed out the passenger side and almost hit the ground as her knees buckled. She sank back into the seat to marshal her strength and wait for the shaking to stop.

When she finally gathered herself together enough to get out of the car, she shivered. Pulling the edges of her coat more tightly around her, she watched Reese talk with the officers. As she approached them, his eye caught hers. Frustration glinted in them. Her heart dropped. "He got away?"

"Yeah. He lost them on a curve."

Maggie didn't have enough energy to be upset. She felt drained, wiped out, empty. An effect of the ebbing of the adrenaline rush, she felt sure.

Reese caught her fingers in his. "Come on. Let's let them worry about this guy for a while. Eli's going to fax over another copy of the bank robber's picture. They'll be watching for him. As for us, we have a dinner to eat."

She stared up at him. "You still want to go?"

"Absolutely." The firm set of his jaw said he wasn't going to let the harrowing mountain ride ruin the evening. Some of her energy began to seep back in.

Reese hung up the phone, pulled into the restaurant parking lot and cut the engine. He'd called Eli to fill him in about the accident. Once Eli was satisfied no one was hurt, he'd given Reese an update on the robbery investigation. Reese planned to give Maggie the details, but first asked, "You okay?"

Maggie drew in a deep breath. "I think so. You?"

He nodded. "Come on. Let's get a table and I'll tell you what Eli said."

They headed toward the entrance and Maggie breathed in the night air. "It'll be Thanksgiving soon," she said.

"I know. Next week."

They stepped inside and Reese gave his name to the hostess, who led them to a table for two at the back of the restaurant. Maggie smiled and he thought he caught sight of a small dimple in her right cheek. "This is nice," she said as she took in the log cabin atmosphere.

"They have amazing steaks. Eli brought me out here about a year ago. I'd just recovered from a gunshot wound and—"

"You were shot?" Shock rippled across her face.

"Yeah. It's a long story, but my sister-in-law, Abby, was in trouble, and I was trying to warn her. By the time I got out here, trouble had already found her and he shot me for good measure."

"Oh, my goodness."

"I know. So anyway, after I recovered, before I went back to Washington, Eli brought me here. Told me I needed to slow down and move to a small town."

Maggie lifted a brow as the waitress filled their water glasses. After several minutes studying their menus, Maggie asked, "What did you say to that?"

"I laughed at him."

"And yet here you are."

Reese gave a rueful chuckle as he remembered that

day. "I think Eli and God had a conversation that I wasn't privy to at the time."

Maggie was quiet for a moment as she studied the table. Then looked up at him. "How do you feel about God after everything you've been through?"

Reese was glad for the brief interruption as the waitress took their order. After she left, he said, "At first I was really angry with God. Blamed Him, blamed Abby, blamed everyone I thought had a part in Keira and Emma's deaths." He sighed. "I was so sure I had a right to seek revenge, but through that whole process of blaming Abby I found I didn't like myself very much. Anger was eating me up inside. Fortunately, I recognized what it was doing to me and was able to find forgiveness and peace."

She looked shocked at his confession. "That doesn't sound like you."

"It wasn't me." He frowned and sighed. "It's difficult to explain, but in my quest for answers, God showed me that wasn't what He had planned for me. He showed me that I was designed for more than that. That I had a purpose, a reason for being here. And one of those reasons was to help save Abby. Once I was able to focus on that, my heart changed."

He saw her swallow hard and wondered if he should have bared so much of his soul. Would it send her running? He tensed as he gave her time to process everything. Then she gave him a gentle smile, the empathy and concern shining in her eyes making him relax. She said, "That's quite a testimony."

"It's just what happened." He took a sip of water. "I'd rather hear about you. Will you tell me what happened with you and your husband?"

She studied him for a moment and he wondered if she'd let him change the subject. Then she shrugged. "At first, I was just dumbfounded that he'd turned out to be an abuser. I couldn't believe he'd managed to hide that part of himself the entire time we dated and were engaged. That I hadn't seen something to set off warning bells in my head. But there was nothing. Even now, looking back at that time, I can't think of anything he might done that I should have noticed as...off." She twisted her fingers and placed her elbows on the table. Settling her chin in her palms, she sighed. "Of course, I realized at some point that he was pushing the relationship along at a pretty fast clip, but..." She shook her head, the confusion on her face snagging his heart and giving it a twist. "But I have to say, I just went along with him. I couldn't believe someone like Kent was interested in me. And—" she swallowed hard "—I was lonely. I let him sweep me off my feet." She gave a grimace.

"So how do you feel about finding someone else? Trusting again?" He tensed, waiting for her answer.

A flush crept into her cheeks. "I think the right man could convince me to try again." Then the flush faded and she said, "I made a really bad choice the first time. I won't do that again." She stared into his eyes. "The right man would have to be patient, take things slow and prove himself." A shrug lifted her shoulders. "I hate that I feel that way, but I guess I just don't know that I trust myself. My judgment. If I could be so wrong before, where do I find the discernment to know that I won't make the same kind of mistake again?"

Reese gave a slow nod. "I guess I can understand why you would feel that way."

"You can?" She seemed surprised.

"Sure. People do it all the time. Not just in relationships like a marriage, but any kind of situation where you're required to make a judgment call or a decision. When you make the wrong one, it's hard to trust that you'll make the right one next time you're faced with the same choice. And now it's not just you who'll be affected by your decision. You have Belle to think of, too."

Maggie dropped her eyes to the plate that the waitress set in front of her, and he could almost see her mind spinning.

For the next several minutes after Reese said the blessing, they ate in comfortable silence.

Then Maggie said, "You haven't filled me in on what Eli had to say about the robbery."

Reese nodded. "They caught the owner of the getaway vehicle."

"Really? Did he tell them the name of the man you shot?"

"Not yet. They caught him in Asheville, but they're bringing him to Bryson City and we're going to play him and Berkley off against each other."

"What do you mean?"

Reese smiled at her as anticipation threaded through him. "Just a little cop game that usually nets some pretty good results. We let them 'accidentally' see each other in the station and then let them know that each of them is being questioned individually. At some point, we usually have enough info on one that we can 'let it slip' to the other that his partner is squealing on him and if he wants to make a deal, now's the time to spill it."

She smiled at him, the admiration in her gaze making him feel ten feet tall. She nodded. "Clever."

"One of the oldest tricks in the book, but it still works when it's done right."

She frowned and Reese could see her mind working. "But that means that it wasn't him who tried to run us off the parkway."

"No, I'm guessing it was his buddy—the one I shot."

"Wounded, but not hurt badly enough to need time to recover."

Reese lifted a brow. "Exactly."

"So he's alone and out for revenge—or he simply wants to shut us up so we don't testify when his partners go to trial."

"Right."

He glanced out the window behind Maggie—a window he made sure was far enough to her left that no one outside could see her sitting at the table—and saw the Rose Mountain cruiser sitting in the parking lot. Probably Mitchell or the new guy, Jason. He smiled. Eli was making sure he had backup should anything else happen on the way home.

His smile slipped into a frown. Maybe this had been a bad idea. From a safety standpoint. Then he looked at the woman across from him, her soft blond hair falling over her shoulders, her delicate lashes fanning her cheeks, and he couldn't regret the time alone with her.

When they'd finished their dinner, Reese felt that he had a better grasp of Maggie and what made her tick. He didn't think he had the whole picture, but at least he had one that wasn't so blurry.

She wanted to trust him, trust her judgment that he was a good guy, but she was still unsure, still hesitant to take that leap of faith yet. And he didn't blame her. He would have his work cut out for him to prove he wasn't like her dead husband. And while he was proving that, he had to find a way to make sure he kept her safe.

He drew in a deep breath. "What do you think about moving to a safe house until we catch this guy?"

ELEVEN

Maggie stepped into her house and shut the door behind her. Full of emotions and feelings from the date—and it *had* been a date—she'd decided against inviting Reese inside. Especially after that question he'd dropped on her at supper. A safe house?

She didn't think so. At least not yet.

He seemed to understand what was going on inside her and hadn't pushed. Instead, he'd made sure there was no awkward moment on the front porch. He'd simply hugged her and said, "I enjoyed the time with you. Sleep well." He'd gestured to the cruiser now in his spot at the end of her driveway. "You've got a good watchdog, rest easy."

She'd nodded and smiled and wondered how she would sleep tonight. Without Belle in the house. Fiona had called to say Belle had fallen asleep, and she was welcome to leave her there for the night. She'd also offered, "You can come here for the night, if you want."

Maggie thought about it. "No, someone's after me, Fiona. I wouldn't feel right about staying with you. I might just bring a truck full of trouble to your door if I do that."

Fiona had simply laughed. "Wouldn't be the first time." Then she'd sobered. "I understand. Belle will be safe here, I promise."

Cal would drop her off on his way in to work in the morning. Maggie had mixed feelings about leaving her daughter there, but, truthfully, she wondered if Belle wasn't safer on Fiona's ranch than in the little house with Maggie.

The question tore at her. And if she hadn't been so conflicted, she would have gone right over to the ranch and picked Belle up. But she wanted her baby to be safe. And the fact was, she might be safer away from her mother.

Maggie sank onto the couch, pushed that depressing thought away and let her mind drift to Reese. The man intrigued her, drew her…and scared her. Not in a physical way, as Kent had, but on a deeper, emotional level. He could be dangerous to her heart.

The phone rang.

Maggie snatched it from the end table. "Hello?"

"I'm not going away."

At first, she didn't understand the whispery voice. "What?"

"I'll be back. No one can protect you from me."

Maggie's thumb pressed the button to hang up the phone. She pressed it twice for good measure. Trembling, her heart thudding from the sudden adrenaline rush, she checked the caller ID.

Private call.

She stood on shaky legs and walked to the window to look out. The cruiser still sat there at the end of her driveway.

Walking into the kitchen, she checked the door, then each room of the house, one by one. All were fine. The bathrooms were empty. No one was hiding in her house. The phone call had her spooked. Her heart still raced and her palms were slick with sweat.

She dialed Reese's number with one hand and peered out at the cruiser once again. She didn't want to go outside and expose herself, even if the cop car was just a few steps from her door.

"Hello?"

"Reese, I just got a phone call that worries me."

His tone sharpened. "What did he say?"

"'I'll be back. No one can protect you from me.'" Just saying the words made the trembling start anew.

A harsh mutter came through the line. Then he said, "I see why you're scared. All right, I'm going to get Eli to see if he can trace the number that called you. Is Jason still outside?"

"Yes."

"I'm going to give him a heads-up and tell him to come inside with you. Then I'm going to talk to Eli. I'll get back to you."

"Okay." She hated the fear that came through that one small word.

"Hey." His voice softened. "You're going to be okay."

Tears threatened. "I know. Thanks, Reese."

"I enjoyed tonight, Maggie."

That made her smile. "I did, too."

He hung up, and she slowly placed the phone on the counter. Deputy White knocked on the door within a minute. She let him in and he scoured the house again. She wasn't surprised that he insisted on searching and came up empty, too. She supposed searching her house by herself had been rather stupid. What if there *had* been someone inside?

Her phone rang again.

She jumped and this time checked the caller ID. Relief swept through her when she saw Shannon's number. "Hello?"

"Oh, Maggie, I'm so glad I got you. My reservation at

the B and B fell through. I need a place to stay. Could I use your spare room?"

Maggie hesitated. She wouldn't mind having Shannon there, but... "Shannon, someone seems to be trying to hurt me. A bank robber has threatened me. I don't know that you'll be safe here."

A pause. "Well, there's safety in numbers, right? Plus you have a cop sitting outside your house. I'm not worried about it."

Maggie fidgeted, wondering if she dared allow Shannon to stay. If something happened to the woman while she was here... "I don't know..."

"Please? I don't have anywhere else to go tonight. Tell the nice deputy that I'm coming so he won't shoot me, okay?"

Maggie sighed. With Shannon, it was always easier to give in than to argue. "Okay, fine. I'll see you soon."

Shannon's knock on the door came thirty minutes later. Maggie answered it and stared at her sister-in-law in surprise. The woman looked a bit more worn than she had before Maggie left with Reese for supper. "Are you okay?"

"Oh, yeah, just very tired and a little frustrated." Shannon rolled her suitcase inside and waved a hand. "When I got to the B and B, they had apparently lost my reservation. Or given it to someone else—or something. Thanksgiving is just a week away and they're filled to capacity."

She placed her hands on her hips and rolled her eyes. "It was too late to find another place to stay."

"So you called me." Maggie smiled, her nerves easing at the woman's presence. Maybe this would be a good idea after all.

"Yes."

"Well, you'll have to take my bedroom. Belle's room is next door and then my office is across the hall."

"Oh, no," Shannon groaned. "I'm putting you out, aren't I?" She grabbed her suitcase handle and the small toiletries bag she'd set on the floor.

As she did, the toiletries bag hit the floor with a thump and the small clasp fell open. Makeup, toothpaste and a small aspirin bottle rolled out. With a grunt, Shannon bent to pick them up. "I'll just drive into that little town that's not too far from here and—"

"Don't be silly," Maggie said as she grabbed the aspirin and handed it Shannon. The woman tucked everything back in the bag and fastened the clasp. Maggie pursed her lips and motioned toward her room. "Go on, I'll be fine. I have a very comfortable daybed in my office." She shrugged. "I spend more time in there than my bedroom anyway."

Shannon continued to look torn and Maggie asked, "You really want to drive to the next town?"

Her sister-in-law shuddered. "No." She pulled the suitcase closer. "Okay, if you're sure."

"I'm sure."

"I'm going job hunting tomorrow. As soon as I get a job, I'll be out of your hair, I promise."

Maggie pointed to her room. "Go."

Shannon didn't hesitate a moment longer. She rolled her suitcase into Maggie's room then darted into the nursery. Maggie followed, curious.

Then watched with amusement as Shannon peered into the crib. Maggie didn't want to laugh at Shannon's disappointment, she knew the woman loved Belle and had missed her over the last few months they'd been gone, but her disgusted expression was quite funny. "She's at a friend's house for the night," Maggie explained.

"Bummer." Shannon pouted. "I wanted to see her."

"I know you did. You can see her tomorrow. My friend

Cal's dropping her off first thing on his way in to work."
An idea occurred to Maggie. "Speaking of seeing Belle.
How would you like to watch her for me while I'm teach-
ing tomorrow?"

Delight lit up Shannon's face. "Are you kidding? I'd
love to. We'll stay right here and play, but we won't get
in your way."

Relief filled Maggie. "Wonderful." Then she frowned.
"But what about your job hunt?"

"Are you crazy? Hunt for a job or take care of my
niece?" She lifted a brow. "Hon, that's a no-brainer."

On impulse, Maggie hugged the woman. "I'm glad
you're here, Shannon, I've missed you."

"Me, too, Maggie. Very glad I'm here." She frowned.
"Although, I should be completely furious with you for
running off without a word."

"I left a note."

"It's not the same thing. I looked for you for a month.
I thought about hiring a private detective, but decided to
wait and see if you called."

Maggie sighed. "I know. And I'm sorry, but I did what
I had to do at the time." She forced a smile. "Forgive me?"

"Maybe." Shannon's lower lip jutted.

Maggie's smile this time was real. "Good night, Shannon."

"Night." Shannon disappeared into Maggie's bedroom.
Maggie had spent the thirty minutes between Shannon's
call and subsequent arrival changing the sheets and clean-
ing the bathroom. Shannon should be fine for the night.

Maggie walked into her office, now her bedroom, and
shut the door. Shannon didn't seem bothered by the police
officer sitting outside Maggie's house or the fact that Maggie had a need for him. And Maggie had to admit that having another adult in the house eased her fears tremendously.

Walking over to her desk, she picked up the envelope she'd meant to mail today and sighed. She'd get it in the mail tomorrow first thing.

Placing the envelope right where she would see it, she laid down on the daybed and closed her eyes.

Worry took over, making them shoot wide open. Would having another woman in the house deter the man who seemed determined to terrorize her into silence? Or would he just go through Shannon to get to Maggie, if that's what it took?

Maggie forced her eyes closed and prayed for safety.

Reese walked into the office the next morning and sat at his desk while he smothered a yawn.

"You know you can come stay with us, don't you?" Cal asked from the doorway.

Reese snapped his jaw shut and sniffed. "I smell coffee. Good coffee. And I know I can. I appreciate the offer, but I want to stay close to Maggie."

The white foam cup appeared in front of him. He snatched it and took a careful swig. "Ahhh. Thanks. My coffeemaker didn't survive the blast." He shook his head. "The bomb goes off in my bedroom, and the coffeemaker takes a hit in the kitchen." He rolled his eyes. "Nothing else in the kitchen. Just the coffeemaker."

"No explaining how or why blasts destroy the things they destroy and leave the things they leave."

"Yeah."

"How's Maggie?"

Reese frowned. "She was all right. I'm getting ready to take my turn watching her house."

"I've got the shift after you."

Reese nodded. "I'm wondering if we should consider moving her to a safer place."

Cal perched himself on the edge of Reese's desk and took a sip of his coffee. "Might not be a bad idea. Got kind of quiet there for a while then the attempt to run you off the road and a threatening call all in one night." He shook his head. "Not good."

"I know." He smiled. "But on the bright side, Maggie's not alone right now. She has a visitor."

"Who?"

"Her former sister-in-law, Shannon Bennett."

"That's good to know. She the one driving that white Mercedes around town?"

"Yep."

"Nice." He paused and his expression turned thoughtful. "She was in the diner last night and caused quite a stir in some of the regulars. Several men were tripping over themselves trying to buy her a drink or her supper."

"It's a small town, where the men outnumber the women by five to one. She's bound to stir things up as long as she's here."

"Better keep our eyes open."

"And our backs to the wall," Reese grunted.

Maggie turned off her computer and stretched. Wednesday was her busiest day with four classes practically back to back, time for a quick lunch then two more classes. Her stomach rumbled, and she glanced at the clock. Time to think about dinner.

She could hear Shannon singing a silly song about horses and cowgirls to Belle. The two had hit it right off the minute Cal had dropped Belle at the house this morning. Maggie had watched them for a little while and then gone to work with a smile.

She'd joined them for lunch, then heard Shannon in Belle's room rocking the baby to sleep. All in all, Maggie felt good about the situation. Good enough to wonder if Shannon might consider doing this for a while.

At least until she found another job.

If she intended to find one. She still couldn't believe Shannon had quit her job back in Spartanburg. She thought she'd planned to just take a leave of absence or some vacation time.

Belle was still sleeping, and Maggie found Shannon in the den reading a novel. "Would you like to stay for Thanksgiving?" she found herself asking.

Shannon looked up, surprise on her face. Then pleasure. "I'd love it."

Maggie felt warmth start to thaw the area around her heart. Shannon really did seem different than when she'd last been around her. Softer, more content. Happy.

"Great." Then she frowned. "What about your parents? Won't they expect you to be with them?"

A grimace crossed Shannon's face. "My parents. I suppose we need to talk about them."

Maggie lifted a brow. "What do you mean?"

"I told them I was going to be moving to Rose Mountain to be closer to you and Belle, and they flipped."

"Flipped?"

"They weren't happy with me."

"Well—" Maggie gave a soft sigh "—they've never liked me and never wanted anything to do with Belle, so that's not surprising, is it?"

This time it was Shannon's turn to look surprised. "What do you mean? Of course they wanted something to do with Belle. But you're right, they didn't approve of you." She shrugged. "No offense, it's just a fact."

Maggie was beyond taking offense at something she'd known and accepted for years. But to hear they wanted to be part of Belle's life?

"But Kent said—"

Shannon waved off her protest with a sharp jab of her hand. An angry glint sparked in the woman's eyes. "Every word out of my brother's mouth was a lie. Haven't you figured that out yet?"

Maggie sank onto the couch. Yes, she'd figured it out before the first year of her marriage had passed. But his parents... "Then why didn't they ever let me know that they wanted to see her?"

"Because Kent wouldn't let them."

Maggie's jaw dropped. "Wouldn't let them?" She knew she sounded like a parrot, repeating Shannon's words, but shock had frozen her brain.

Shannon shook her head and narrowed her eyes. "Kent needed money. He asked them to give it to him. They wouldn't."

More shock settled over her. She wilted into the pillow behind her. "Money? But we weren't hurting for money. You saw the house we lived in, the car Kent drove." He hadn't allowed her to drive, but spared no expense when it came to his own automobile. Fortunately, they lived within walking distance of a small grocery store. When he left for work, she often went walking, sometimes to the grocery store, sometimes to the small church on the outskirts of the neighborhood.

Shannon gave a small, uncharacteristic snort. "It was all image with him. And, yeah, he made good money as a stockbroker, but he also liked to gamble, and that wasn't a good thing for his bank account."

"Gamble?" Maggie felt the blood drain from her face. "I never really knew him at all, did I?"

"No, unfortunately, you didn't."

Belle's "I'm awake" cry sounded and Shannon jumped

to her feet, the book tumbling onto the floor. "I'll get her," she said as she raced toward the nursery.

In spite of the things she'd just learned about her former in-laws and the disturbing news about Kent, Maggie smiled and shook her head as she picked up the book. It might be nice having Shannon around.

She thought about the envelope still sitting on her desk to be mailed and looked down the hall where Shannon had disappeared into Belle's room.

Maybe she'd wait another couple of days before mailing it after all.

Reese knocked on Deputy White's cruiser window. The glass lowered and Reese caught the man on the tail end of a yawn. "Sorry," White said. "It's just boring as all get out watching this place."

"Wasn't boring a few nights ago."

"Yeah. I know." He said it as if he wished something would happen.

"Reese?"

He turned to see Maggie standing in the doorway. Her flushed cheeks and the white substance on her nose and cheeks said she'd been busy in the kitchen. He tapped the door and said to Jason, "You can take off. I've got the evening covered."

"You don't have to say it twice." Deputy White started the car and left, a spray of gravel spitting up behind him as he turned out of the driveway.

Reese gave the area around him a good look as he walked toward Maggie. He admired her beauty, and wondered what she saw in him. Then decided he didn't care as long as she liked what she saw.

The look in her eyes said she did.

A strange, peaceful feeling flowed through him, taking him by surprise. And making him smile.

"Would you like to join us for dinner?" she asked.

"Shannon's still here?"

"She is."

He swiped a finger down her nose. "What did that belong to?"

Maggie giggled. And his heart did strange things. Things it hadn't done in a very long time. She backed up and motioned him inside, saying, "I made cookies for dessert. I haven't baked in a while and decided we needed some sweets."

"I'm always up for cookies." He followed her into the small foyer and saw Shannon holding Belle. She smiled and he nodded. "I'm glad you're here to keep Maggie company."

"Me, too."

Reese felt the hair on the back of his neck rise. Uneasiness flowed through him and he shivered at the sudden unexpected feeling.

The foyer window shattered inward and Reese felt a sting under his right eye even as he dove for Maggie, heard Shannon scream, and two more bullets pound the wooden door.

TWELVE

Maggie whirled, her first thought to grab Belle and cover her. A hard arm around her waist stopped her midflight and took her to the floor. She cried out. "Belle!"

"Stay here," Reese demanded. Maggie flipped around to see him pull Shannon and Belle to the floor behind the recliner in the den.

He was already reaching for his phone when the glass on the other side of the door mimicked the first one, shattering all over the foyer floor and spraying into the den.

Reese barked, "Shooter at Maggie Bennett's house with a good view of her front door."

Trembling, breaths coming in pants and tears blurring her eyes, she crawled toward Belle and Shannon, her only thought to get to her baby and cover her, protect her.

"Maggie! Stop! Stay still!"

She froze.

And realized she was crawling over the glass on the floor. And her arms were bleeding. "Belle," she cried as she frantically searched for Shannon and the baby.

"She's fine, Maggie. I have her. She's fine," Shannon reassured her. Maggie wasn't reassured. She wanted to see her baby for herself, hold her in her arms and keep her safe.

A bullet hit just above her head. She ducked with a scream.

Glass crunched under Reese's feet as he moved toward her. What was he doing? He'd be exposed. She felt him gently grasp her upper arm and pull her up and way from the line of fire. "Down the hall, into the bedroom and under the bed."

She jerked from his grasp. "Not without my baby."

"I'll get Belle and bring her to you, but go."

Three more shots beat a staccato beat against her door, and one whizzed by Reese, who flinched and pulled her down once more. "Go!"

She went. Crying and begging God to spare the life of her child.

And everyone in her house.

Anger, hot and furious flowed through her, drying her tears, fueling her determination, even as she heard footsteps behind her. She turned to see Shannon leading the way, followed by Reese who had Belle tucked up against his chest, shoulders hunched over her.

Maggie slipped into the bedroom and sank to the floor next to the bed, making sure she was out of sight of the window on the opposite wall.

Shannon burst through the door and dropped beside her. Maggie held her arms out for Belle and flinched when Reese hesitated, then handed the crying baby to Shannon. He stumbled back so fast he nearly tripped and fell. Her stomach dipped as she realized how hard it was for him to hold Belle even in this crazy situation. But to give the baby to Shannon, that hurt. Then she saw her outstretched arms and knew why he'd hesitated.

Blood covered her arms from elbow to wrist where she'd tried to crawl army-style across the glass in her foyer.

"We'll get you some medical help soon," he promised.

"I'm fine. I'll be fine." But the trembling wouldn't stop, and the terrible nerve-shattering fear just kept building.

Shannon looked pale, but surprisingly calm as she huddled over a now-screaming Belle. Maggie's heart wrenched at her daughter's angry and scared cries, but with her arms the mess they were, Maggie couldn't do anything but whisper comforting words in her ear.

"I'm going after him," Reese said. "Stay put and stay away from the windows."

"Reese, no! You can't! Not without your backup." She blinked. "Where is your backup? Why are they taking so long to get here?"

"It's not taking them that long," he grunted as he pushed the tall dresser in front of the window. "It just seems like it is when you've got bullets whizzing all around you."

And then he was gone, locking the bedroom door behind him.

The sudden silence made Reese's ears ring. No more bullets came his way, but that didn't mean the shooter was gone. In the foyer, he waited by the door, his gun ready. Where was Jason? When no more shots sounded, he headed for the kitchen door and threw it open, staying off to the side, well clear of the opening.

More silence.

Reese waited then said into his phone, "How far away are you?"

"You should hear us coming in about a minute."

"I'm going after him, Eli."

"Reese…" The warning in Eli's voice didn't deter him.

"He's already stopped shooting. If I wait any longer, he's going to be long gone."

"Where's Jason?"

"Good question." Reese looked out the window and saw the deputy behind his car, weapon drawn. "I see him. The two of us will get started looking for him."

"Where's he shooting from?"

He looked across the lake. "My house." Reese stiffened as he saw a lone figure racing along the edge of his property, a rifle clutched in his right hand. Reese shoved his Bluetooth piece into his ear and kept his phone on so Eli could hear what was going on. "I see him. He's at the edge of the lake. I'm using the trees for cover."

Over the radio, Reese said, "Jason, watch the house."

"Copy that." Jason's voice sounded a bit wobbly. Could be he'd gotten a little more excitement than he'd wanted. *Lord, don't let him get shot.*

Slipping the phone into his pocket, he kept his eyes on the figure who still moved along the edge of the lake.

He was heading this way, toward Maggie's house, not away from it. Coming to check and make sure his bullets hit home?

Reese frowned at the man's uneven gait. He kept weaving, unsteady, losing his footing every now and then.

Now at the top of the semicircle the cove made, the shooter kept up his awkward pace and came toward Maggie's house at a good clip, then stumbled and went down on one knee. He got up and continued on the same path. Coming straight toward Reese, who stayed hidden in the edge of the trees.

Then the silence was broken by the sound of sirens in the distance. Eli was on his way. Jason had the house covered. Maggie, Belle and Shannon were safe as long as Reese had eyes on the shooter. The man stopped, and Reese finally got a good look at him. The one named Slim. His indecision was plain to see from where Reese stood.

Keeping to the trees at the top of the property, Reese started making his way toward the shooter. Soon he would be in the exposed grassy area that led toward the muddy area of the lake.

Then Slim was moving again, having come to an apparent decision on what he planned to do.

And that was to run.

Reese quit trying to be quiet and took off after the now-fleeing shooter, leaving the cover of the trees and praying Slim didn't turn and start taking shots at him. Slim probably had a car waiting near Reese's house and wanted to get back to it now that he could hear that help was on the way. Reese felt sure that the man hadn't planned on leaving anyone alive to call the cops. Fortunately, Slim didn't seem to be such a great shot.

Heart thumping, Reese heard his feet pounding over the hard ground. He broke through the dense tree line, playing tag with the trees scattered along the edge of the crescent-shaped shoreline, using them for cover as he kept pursuing the fleeing figure. Slim glanced back over his shoulder, and Reese was close enough to see determination stamped on the man's features.

Then he stumbled and went down. Propped himself up and tried to keep going. Fell again, then turned the gun on Reese who came within thirty yards. Reese darted behind the nearest tree as he lifted his weapon and yelled, "Freeze! Drop your gun!"

Slim slung the rifle around and pulled the trigger. Bark flew from the tree, and Reese flinched as he felt his cheek sting. As the man took a few precious seconds to aim for a better shot, Reese squeezed the trigger. Slim screamed and went down, his rifle landing beside him as he clutched his leg.

Reese looked over his shoulder to see Eli and backup racing toward him. Keeping his weapon trained on the man now writhing on the ground, he strode to him and kicked the rifle out of reach.

As Slim cried out his agony, Reese stated, "You're

under arrest. You have the right to remain silent." As Reese quoted him the Miranda rights, another siren bit through the winter air. An ambulance, guided by Eli on the phone, headed their way. Fortunately, the injured party was the one on the ground and not any of his intended victims.

As Eli reached his side, Reese holstered his weapon. Eli patted the suspect down and came up with nothing but a piece of paper with a phone number on it in the man's left front pocket.

Reese pulled his cell phone out and called the number.

"Anything?" Eli asked.

"Straight to voice mail. Phone's turned off and the voice mail is an automated one."

EMTs approached on Eli's signal and went straight to the moaning man. Cal stood next to him to make sure he didn't try anything, but Reese didn't think he had the ability to do much. The bright flush on the shooter's cheeks and the harsh panting breaths didn't fit with the short sprint along the edge of the lake.

"Reese, are you okay?"

He turned to see Maggie jogging toward him, concern and fear on her face.

The blood on her arms was still there. He said, "I'm fine, but let's get you looked at." Reese gestured toward one of the EMTs, who came over. "Can you take a look at her arms?"

She flushed. "They look worse than they are, I think. They just sting really bad." She frowned. "You're bleeding."

He lifted a hand to his cheek. "It's nothing. We need to get your arms taken care of."

A protest still on her lips and concern in her eyes, she walked with the paramedic toward the truck, Reese close on her heels. When they passed the man who'd tried to kill her, she came to a stop and looked down at him. The shooter met her gaze and smirked through his pain. Maggie's expression didn't change. She simply stared at him.

It seemed to unnerve him. "What?" Slim gritted out.

"Was it worth it?"

Confusion flickered in his bloodshot eyes. "What are you talking about?"

"The bank robbery. Trying to kill us? Possibly killing a baby. Everything. Was it worth it?"

He grunted then glared. "If you hadn't interfered, everything would have gone as planned. And yeah, it would have been worth it."

Maggie didn't flinch, didn't blink, didn't move. She simply stared as she processed the man's words. Reese frowned, wondering what was going through her head. Then she said, "But you got away. You could have kept going and never looked back. You could have hit another bank and probably gotten away with the money. Why keep coming after us? Why take a chance on getting caught when you knew I had deputies watching my every move?"

He shut his mouth and looked away.

"What's your name?"

"None of your business."

Maggie didn't budge, just kept her gaze on the man.

Again, her unwavering stare seemed to make him uncomfortable and he sighed, then coughed, a harsh hacking cough. A groan escaped him and he said, "I'm in the system. All you gotta do is run my prints."

"So what's your name?" she pressed.

"Doug Patterson. Can I have some water?"

Reese wrapped his hand around Maggie's upper arm and gently pulled her toward the waiting paramedic. This time, Maggie didn't protest, but the frown between her brows remained.

"We got him. It's over."

A laugh sounded from behind him. He turned to see the EMT working on Patterson, but the man's hard eyes said he had something else to say. Reese lifted a brow in his direction.

"Over?" Patterson gave a humorless snort then licked his dry chapped lips. "You think this is over? You ruined the chance of a lifetime for me," he snarled. "It's far from over. A lot of money was lost on this job." Fury turned his blue eyes to chips of ice. "And my boss isn't going to let it just be over. So you'd better watch your back and sleep with one eye open."

"Shut up!" Shannon yelled as she stomped toward them, Belle in her arms. "Just shut up! How can you do this to people? To a baby? You could have killed her!"

Reese stepped in between Shannon and the man now glaring at her. She looked mad enough to do him bodily damage. Belle sucked on her pacifier and seemed content until she spotted Maggie with the EMT. Belle let out a cry and held her arms out toward Maggie.

Reese reluctantly took the baby from a glowering Shannon and walked over to Maggie. Another officer led a still-furious and vocal Shannon away.

Belle squirmed in Reese's arms, wanting her mother. Maggie looked at Belle and crooned, "Just a minute, baby."

Her wounds didn't look as bad as he'd feared when he first saw all the blood. Now that they were almost cleaned up, he could see that the cuts weren't too deep. As the EMT began to bandage the worst ones, he concentrated on soothing Belle, knowing his attempts were awkward and unwanted.

Screeching, Belle strained against him and lunged for Maggie. Reese prayed the paramedic would hurry up.

Maggie finally pushed the helping hands away with an apology and reached for Belle.

Reese let her go, the heat from her small body nearly singeing his palms. The baby quieted the moment her mother's arms closed around her. Maggie placed a kiss on her daughter's forehead and whispered soothing words in her tiny ear. Reese's heart jerked in his chest, and he swallowed hard. What would it be like to be on the receiving end of Maggie's love?

The thought nearly overwhelmed him and he turned away to concentrate on what he needed to do to get information out of the now-subdued Patterson.

Subdued due to pain medication. Reese wanted to jerk the IV out of the man's arm.

The EMT working on him looked at Reese. "This guy has a bad infection in his left shoulder. Looks like it's from a previous gunshot wound. He's got a fever and is one sick dude."

"Yeah, well, today's not the first time I've shot him."

The EMT lifted a brow. "Ooo-kay."

Reese didn't bother to explain as they loaded Patterson into the back of the ambulance. Cal holstered his weapon and said, "I'll go with him."

"I'm going to get Maggie and Shannon settled back inside the house." He looked at Eli. "Then we've got to talk."

Eli nodded. "Yeah, because while we've caught all the robbers, this is obviously not over."

"Exactly."

Maggie paced the floor of her kitchen, her sneakers making a squeaking noise on the linoleum with each step. It wasn't over. Why not?

Reese said to give him a few minutes to finish things up and he'd be in. He'd also called someone to come over to patch up the window that had been shattered by the bullets. Maggie had gotten Belle to sleep with very little trouble, but she was afraid the hammering and banging would soon wake her. She'd practically had to pry the baby out of Shannon's arms to put her to sleep. "But I haven't seen her in six months," she'd whined. "I'm playing catch-up for all the time I lost with her and she's had a rough night. Let me put her down."

"No." Maggie had needed to hold Belle, needed her reassuring weight in her arms, her soft baby breath blowing on her neck. "She needs her mother tonight."

So Shannon had agreed with a grimace then glanced at her watch and gave a low shriek. "I've got to go."

"What? Where?" Maggie frowned. How could the woman think about going somewhere after all that had happened?

But Shannon was already in her bedroom.

Maggie shook her head and walked into the kitchen. She peered into the refrigerator and wondered what she would fix for dinner. But she didn't want any food right now. What she wanted was a nap.

Shannon entered the kitchen, hair swept up into a professional bun. She wore a knee-length skirt and a white blouse and brown blazer. Matching brown pumps completed her outfit. Maggie stared. "What are you all dressed up for?"

"I have a meeting in Bryson City. I'm thinking of getting a job nearby so I'm heading over there to talk to the CEO of an advertising firm there. Guess it's time to see if I can put my degree to work again." She shrugged. "I don't have to work, of course, but what will I do all day without a job?" She held up a hand as though to forestall any protestations. "Don't worry, I'll help you out with Belle until then, but I need to find a job or I'll be bored silly."

"Oh." Maggie blinked. "All right. Do you want to eat first? I was just thinking about fixing something."

"No, thanks. It's a dinner interview. I may be late."

With a wave and a smile, she turned on her heel and went out the door.

Relieved to have some time for herself to just think, Maggie's brain tumbled like crazy as she'd rocked Belle to sleep.

Once Belle was down, Maggie grabbed a quick shower. Coming out of the bathroom, weariness tugged at her. Her bed tempted her. She sighed and rubbed her eyes. She'd like nothing more than to curl up on her own bed, pull the covers over her head and hide from the world.

But she couldn't. Because something kept niggling at her. She pulled her still-damp hair up in a ponytail and walked into her office. She spent the next forty-five minutes working on school paperwork to prepare for the three meetings she had next week.

Maggie shivered. The hole in her window had been covered with plastic, but it was still cold in the house. She hoped the window was fixed fast.

A knock on her door pulled her from the computer and into the foyer. She opened the door to find Reese standing there looking battle-worn and tired. "Hi."

"Hi." He held up several bags of food.

She inhaled and her stomach rumbled. "I smell something good."

"I didn't figure you felt much like putting together anything, so I had one of Holly's helpers bring this out."

Touched by his thoughtful gesture, she opened the door wider. "You seem to like bringing food to my house."

He lifted a brow and smiled. "Gives me an excuse to see you."

Maggie felt the flush rise on her cheeks. "You don't need

an excuse. And don't worry, I'm not complaining. I appreciate it. Come on in." She took the bags into the kitchen, set them on the counter and said, "Come with me."

At his questioning look, she pointed to his cheek. "You never had anyone clean that up, did you?"

He raised his hand and touched the wound, surprise in his eyes. "No, I guess not. I forgot about it."

"I have a first aid kit in my bathroom. Let's wash that before it gets infected."

"I can take care of it later."

She paused and looked into his eyes. "Reese, I can't stop bank robbers and I can't chase down men with guns, and I can't even do much to protect myself against someone who wants to hurt me and Belle." She bit her lip. "But this is one thing I can do for you. Will you let me?"

At her gentle question, his expression turned tender. He gave a slow nod. "Sure."

He followed her into the master bedroom and on into the bathroom where he seated himself on the edge of the tub. "It's cold in here. Are you sure Belle's warm enough?"

Maggie smiled. "I put the little portable heater in her room. She's fine."

Maggie opened the small linen closet, pulled out the hard plastic box that held all her first aid items and placed it next to the sink. She held a washcloth under the warm water and felt Reese's eyes following her every movement.

It made her extremely self-conscious, and her fingers trembled as she held the washcloth to the wound, soaking away the dried blood. His hand came up to cover hers and he said, "Thank you."

Her smile felt shaky, but she forced it wider. "Sure." She pulled the washcloth away and tossed it into the dirty clothes basket. After applying some antibiotic cream, she opened a small bandage and placed it over the cut. His hands came up to rest on her shoulders, his face inches from hers.

All of a sudden the bathroom felt too small, his size dwarfing her, his presence surrounding her. His right hand slid from her shoulder to cup her chin. Then he leaned down and placed his lips over hers. A gentle caress filled with gratitude, comfort...and a restrained passion.

She went still, savoring his nearness, the security he represented, relishing everything about him. When he lifted his head, she simply stared up at him. He gave a small sigh. "I've been wanting to do that for a while now, but was afraid if I did you'd smack me."

Maggie couldn't help the smile that slid across her tingling lips. "I'm not going to complain."

Full-fledged laughter rumbled from his chest and he pulled her close for a hug. She rested her head against him. "Thank you for all you're doing, Reese. If it wasn't for you, I don't know what—"

His finger over her lips cut her off. "I wouldn't want to be anywhere else."

Maggie nodded. Another rumble sounded and she giggled. "Are you hungry?"

"Starved," he admitted with a self-conscious quirk to his lips.

She closed the first aid kit and opened the linen closet once again. She moved aside a few towels and placed the box on the shelf.

Then Reese looked up, studying her. "You okay?"

"I will be." Maybe. When time passed and this was all behind her. Assuming she was still alive at that point. Together, they walked into the kitchen.

"I need to ask you a few questions," he said.

She frowned. "Okay."

"I've been thinking about something for about the past thirty minutes."

"What's that?"

"Your husband's murder."

THIRTEEN

He saw her flinch and regretted the lack of finesse in his delivery. Reese rushed to apologize. "I'm sorry. Let me back up a bit."

She waved his apology away as she set the food on the table. Maggie waited while Reese said grace then asked, "It's all right. What do you want to know?"

"I've been going over and over this bank robbery in my mind. Plus I've watched the security videos. I've played it scene by scene. The robbery, your response. My response. And something keeps nagging at me."

"What?"

"That's the problem. I don't know. I always say the best way to solve a case is good investigative work and listening when your gut sends you warning signals. My gut is sending signals and is telling me to find out more information about your husband and the possible suspects involved. Will you tell me what happened? Everything you remember about the night he died? Who the police questioned—everything."

Maggie wiped nonexistent crumbs from the table and sighed. "You could look it up. It's all in the police report."

"I want to hear it from you. You'll give me stuff I can't get from the file."

Maggie glanced down the hall toward the nursery and he figured she was calculating how much time she had before the baby woke. "Fine." She paused to take a bite of her sandwich.

While she nibbled at her food, Reese devoured his. He couldn't remember if he'd had lunch or not.

He ate the last fry on his plate and studied her. She appeared fragile on the outside, but he'd witnessed her inner strength more than once. He realized that he admired her.

Once they were finished, she placed the dishes in the dishwasher while he tossed the empty food bags. She turned to say something.

And Belle hollered for attention.

Maggie snapped her mouth shut and started for the hall. Reese snagged her arm and took a deep breath as he felt the words hover on the tip of his tongue. He finally spit them out. "Let me."

Before she had a chance to ask all the questions brewing in her eyes, he was down the hall and in the nursery.

Belle wasn't unhappy. She was just awake and ready to get out of the crib. And Reese figured she probably needed a diaper change. When he'd found out Keira was pregnant, he'd read everything he could get his hands on about pregnancy and the first year with a baby. If he remembered correctly, the books said to change the baby upon waking.

"Hey, there, Belle, did you have a good nap?"

Her brown eyes went wide, then she smiled at him and his heart stuttered a beat.

Reese took a deep breath then slipped his hands under the small arms and picked her up. Then grimaced. Yep, the books were right on. A change would be the first order of business.

He laid her on the changing table and got to work while

he talked to her. "Wish I could take a nap. You have it easy, kid. Hope you appreciate all your mom does for you."

She waved a tiny fist at him and he caught it, staring at the perfect miniature. Small, perfect fingers and a beautifully shaped hand. Delicate. Fragile. Breakable.

And yet strong. Just like her mother.

Belle tried to roll off the table and Reese held her, keeping her in place. Keeping her safe. "Can't do that darling," he said. "You'd land on the floor and that would hurt."

He shuddered at the thought of her being hurt. By accident or by someone who didn't believe life was a precious gift and was willing to snatch it away. He fastened the first tab on the diaper, pulled her other leg down and managed to close the diaper and fasten the second tab. "Practicing on dolls doesn't compare to the actual experience. Dolls don't wriggle. You were a tough customer, sweetheart."

He leaned over the baby and stared her in the eye, face to face, nose to nose. Belle went still as a rock, looking at him as if she wondered if he'd done everything right and if she dared move. He gave a low laugh, his heart light for the first time since he'd seen Maggie and Belle in the bank. "You're awfully cute."

As though she understood, Belle grinned, her brown eyes sparkling. Reese decided at that moment he'd never get his heart back.

Tears flooded Maggie's eyes. Without a moment's hesitation, she snatched the camera she'd left on Belle's small table by the door and snapped a picture.

Still resting on his forearms, Reese looked over his shoulder and smiled. "What? You checking up on me? You think I need some help corralling a mere fifteen pounds of baby?"

His teasing words chased the tears away, and she

shrugged, "Maybe." Reese straightened and pulled Belle into his arms. To Maggie's surprise, the baby seemed happy to be there. And Reese seemed fine having her there. "She's nine months old today."

He lifted a brow. "I'm guessing time goes fast."

Maggie nodded. "Very."

Belle kicked her legs and caught Reese in the stomach. He grunted. "I think she's going to be a soccer player."

"You would have been a great dad," Maggie whispered the words.

Reese stilled. Then a huge sigh filtered from him and he dropped his head. Maggie wished she could snatch the words back. Then he lifted his head, a sad smile on his face. "I sure would have done my best."

Relieved that her words hadn't plunged him into the depths of sadness, Maggie nodded toward the den. "While Shannon is gone, you want to have that conversation?"

"Sure." He handed Belle to her and she started down the hall to the den.

Reese rubbed his head and said. "Hey, do you mind if I help myself to a couple of those aspirin I saw in your medicine cabinet?"

She turned back to face him. Concern immediately clouded her eyes. "Of course I don't mind. I'll get them for you."

"I can get them." He smiled and headed to her bedroom. Once inside her bathroom, he opened the medicine cabinet and saw the bottle of aspirin sitting on the shelf to the side. He helped himself to two, almost took them, then stopped. They didn't look right. Small round yellow tablets. He frowned and put the bottle back. Carrying the pills, he walked into the kitchen to find Maggie preparing a bottle for Belle. "Hey, these were in your aspirin bottle, but I don't think they're aspirin."

Her brows pulled together in a frown as she studied the little yellow pills. "I've never seen those before. They must belong to Shannon."

Still frowning, he said, "I'll put them back. Just be careful when you go to get some aspirin."

"Okay."

Reese put the bottle back where he found it and returned to the kitchen to find Maggie standing there with a glass of tea and two little white pills. "I had these in my purse. I know for a fact that these are aspirin."

He smiled his thanks and downed the two pills.

The door opened and shut and Reese saw Shannon stomp into the foyer. She paused when she saw him, turned on her heel and started down the hall.

Maggie lifted a brow in his direction and went after her sister-in-law. Keeping her voice low so she wouldn't wake up Belle, he heard her ask, "Shannon? What's wrong?"

"Nothing. Just...nothing."

"Something is," he heard Maggie insist.

"My plans...changed." A thud sounded and he imagined her tossing a shoe. "I sat there and waited and waited and he stood me up. Not even a stinking phone call." He heard the woman blow out a disgusted sigh followed by another thud. "I'm just upset that I can't do anything about it. Don't worry about it, I'll get over it."

"I'm sorry. There's some food in the fridge. There was plenty, and we couldn't eat it all."

"Thanks. I'm going to go change first."

Maggie returned to the den where Reese now sat on the couch. She took the bottle of juice she'd carried with her from the kitchen and set it on the end table, then perched on the edge of the recliner, her eyes serious, face thoughtful as she tapped one foot against the floor. Belle sat in the exersaucer, bouncing and slapping at the various toys attached to the device.

Reese watched Maggie's restlessness with compassion. He hated making her relive what he could tell were some pretty awful days. He seated himself on the couch. "Tell me about Kent's job, his habits, who he hung around with."

"Why?"

"Because someone's after you. It may be related to the bank robbery—or it may be something else."

She lifted a brow. "You think whoever killed him would wait six months to come after me? What would be the purpose of that?"

"I don't know." He stood and walked over to place his hands on her shoulders. "I'm just saying we need to consider everything. I don't want to be blindsided, surprised because I ignored my gut. Sometimes what seems obvious..."

"...isn't?"

"Yes. Exactly."

Maggie bit her lip. "His and Shannon's parents didn't like me. They made no effort to be even halfway civil to me. They had in mind the girl they wanted him to marry. But for some reason, he wasn't interested." She snorted. "Well, I know now why he wasn't interested. He knew he couldn't browbeat her—" She chopped her sentence off and looked away.

Reese felt his gut clench and hastened to reassure her. "You were vulnerable, Maggie. Kent saw that and used it to his advantage. It's not your fault."

She blinked away the tears and nodded. "I know that now." A sniff and a sigh and she had herself back under control. "So anyway, he was home a lot at first after we were married, but then I guess I started to bore him and he...um, found other ways to alleviate the boredom."

"He had a girlfriend?"

"Girlfriends," she whispered.

Reese clenched a fist and wished he could plant it in the dead man's face. "How did he die?"

"A hit-and-run car accident."

"Only it wasn't an accident."

She blinked. "No. There was a witness, a homeless man who said he saw a man arguing with someone. He said the person Kent was arguing with stayed inside the car, so he couldn't see the person. But then Kent slammed a fist on the hood of the car. He shouted something like 'That's final. That's the way it's going to be, get over it.' And then started to walk away. The car with the other person accelerated and slammed into him. Kent died instantly. The car never stopped after it hit him."

Reese rubbed his eyes. "I'm sorry, Maggie."

"I don't know who could have done that. One of the women he strung along. An irate husband or boyfriend. Someone he punched out in a bar." She shrugged and shook her head. "It could have been any of a hundred people, Reese. There's just no way to tell."

"I don't suppose your homeless guy got a license plate?"

She gave a humorless laugh. "No. He just said it was a green car."

Reese frowned. "Sounds like a crime of passion, of opportunity."

"What do you mean?"

"I mean, it doesn't sound planned, premeditated. Like Kent was supposed to meet with the person in the other car, they had an argument and the person didn't like what he had to say and acted in a fit of anger or rage."

"Maybe."

"Or not." He shrugged. "It's all speculation, but I'm really wondering if all this doesn't have something to do with his murder."

"Why are you going through all this? Why don't you just let Kent rest in peace?" Shannon spoke from the door, her tone low, voice tight.

Maggie jerked her gaze to her sister-in-law. "Because if Reese is right, connecting Kent to the events going on around me will help us figure out exactly why someone is out to get me."

Shannon sniffed then reached up to rub her eyes. "Are you listening to yourselves? How in the world could Kent's death be linked to what's going on with you?"

Maggie shook her head and looked at Reese. "I don't know. Her question is a good one. How could Kent's death six months ago have anything to do with a bank robbery gone wrong?"

He stood. "I have no idea, but I'm going to find out."

The next morning, Reese sat at his desk working on the paperwork that comes with a shooting. It was being investigated even as he typed.

Eli opened the glass door and a gust of cold air blew in with him. "Hey, guys, let's have a little powwow in the conference room."

Reese lifted a brow at Cal and his friend shrugged. They followed Eli, with Jason bringing up the rear. Mitchell was the deputy assigned to Maggie's house this morning. He'd just called to say Maggie's broken window was fixed and all was well.

Once inside the conference room, Eli shut the door. "Have a seat." He slapped a file folder on the table in front of him. "Well, we've got them all."

Reese felt satisfaction run through him for a brief moment, but that satisfaction quickly turned to concern. Yes, they'd captured all three robbers. But they didn't have the boss. "When do we get to question Patterson?"

"He's at the hospital now. I tried talking to him last night, but he was drugged up and out of it. He's got a nasty infection from your first gunshot wound. Asheville P.D. has a guard on his door. We'll be making a little visit to the hospital shortly."

Reese stood. "I'm going to call Maggie." He stepped outside the conference room and dialed her number.

She answered on the third ring. "Hello?"

"Good morning, pretty lady."

A low laugh reached him. "You sound awfully cheerful this morning."

"Maybe that's because we're getting ready to go over to the hospital to question Patterson."

For a moment, silence filled the line. Then she said, "What about the boss he mentioned? Have you found out anything about him?"

"Not yet, but I've got some ideas I plan to work with as soon I get back to the office. Eli's still going to keep someone on your house. Right now it's White. He was real apologetic for taking this assignment lightly."

"He was?"

"Yeah. He caught me this morning. He apologized several times and promised he'd be vigilant in watching out for you. I believe him."

"Okay, thanks…" She seemed at a loss for words.

"But don't drop your guard yet, Maggie. I don't think Patterson was all hot air when he was saying it's not all over yet."

"I won't." She paused. "Thank you," she whispered. "Thanks for everything."

His throat tightened and he cleared it. "You're welcome."

He hung up and pressed the phone into his forehead while he replayed Patterson's parting comments.

He had a lot of thinking to do.

But first, he wanted to get over to the hospital and talk to the man he'd shot. Because while it was good news that all three robbers were now in custody, Reese couldn't shake the feeling that he was missing something important. Something he needed to put together before someone else got hurt. Or killed.

FOURTEEN

Maggie looked up to see Reese and Eli walking toward the nurses' station. When Reese's eyes landed on her, he couldn't hide his surprise. She shrugged at the unasked question on his face. "I wanted to be here. I want to hear what he has to say."

He looked over her shoulder.

"Jason brought me, but don't be mad at him. I told him I was coming with or without him."

"Maggie—"

"Reese, don't try to talk me out of it. If you'll leave the door open a crack, I can just listen in." She swallowed hard. "That bullet in the bank came real close to my head. The bullets he fired tore up my house and could have killed my daughter. Or you. Or Shannon. He bombed your house partly because of me. I think I have a right to hear him talk."

The men exchanged a look and Reese said, "It's fine with me. If I were in her shoes, I'd be doing the same thing."

Reese blew out a sigh and said to her, "All right. By the door. But you don't say a word, okay?"

She nodded. "Thank you." Maggie followed the men to the prisoner's room. Reese reached up to squeeze her arm and then the two officers entered the room, leaving the door slightly ajar so she could listen in.

"How you feeling, Patterson?"

The man uttered a crude phrase, and Maggie flinched. He was never going to talk. Despair hit her. She wanted to be safe. She wanted to be free to take Belle for a walk down the street without wondering if someone would try to kill her. She wanted—

Reese was speaking again. "You know this would all go easier for you if you'd just tell us the story. Who's the boss you were talking about?"

Maggie inched her head to the right so she could see into the room. She could make out Patterson's feet at the foot of the bed. She could see Reese clearly as he faced the door. Eli had his back to her, but she could see his head and the right part of his body. And if she looked a little to the left, she could see the whole room in the mirror on the far wall. Doug Patterson looked rough. His cheeks were still flushed and he looked like a very sick man.

"No boss. It must have been the fever talking. I don't have a boss." He leaned his head back against the bed and closed his eyes. His throat worked.

Silence as she saw Reese lift his eyes to Eli. There must have been some kind of silent cop communication because Reese dropped his head and nodded. "Right. No boss."

"So…" Eli took a deep breath "…guess we'll just send you up to Marion Correctional Institute."

"Whatever."

"And let it be known that the three of you were trying to kill a baby," Reese stated, his voice low. Lethal.

"What?" Doug's eyes popped open and he stared at the men at the foot of his bed. "No way. Wasn't trying to kill a baby. Are you crazy?" The man protested long and loud. Reese simply stood there. Then shrugged.

"So you say. I don't know that. Do you know that for sure, Eli?"

Eli shook his head. "Nope. Those bullets came awfully close to that baby."

Maggie heard Eli's phone ring over Patterson's protests. Eli pulled it out of his pocket with his right hand and spoke into his phone. "Brody here." He listened as Reese and the prisoner fell quiet. Then Eli let out a short laugh. "Really? They did? Sang like canaries, huh? Thanks for the update."

He hung up and looked at Reese. "We don't need this guy. Station says the two down there are seeing which one can talk the fastest."

"Right," Patterson sneered. "Like I'm going to fall for that."

Eli simply lifted a brow. "So the three of you never met at your father's ranch to work out the deal?"

Uncertainty flared. "No."

"Right. And Compton also said you're the ringleader who was going to deposit ten grand in his account so he could party it up in Mexico."

Full-blown panic crossed his face. "How do you know all that?"

Eli snickered. "Looks like you're going to come up with the short end of the draw." He motioned to Reese. "Let's go."

The men started toward the door and Maggie pulled back.

"No!" Patterson hollered. "Wait! I want a deal. I...I'm not taking the fall for this!"

A slow smile crossed Reese's lips. And he and Eli exchanged smug grins before they wiped them off and turned back to the man in the bed.

Reese shook his head. "I don't know. What do you think you can offer that these guys can't?"

"I was the main contact. I was contacted first and never said anything to those guys about the fact that the robbery was a cover-up."

Maggie saw Reese go still. "A cover-up for what?"

The right foot under the sheet shifted, a restless move that said the prisoner didn't want to say another word. "What kind of deal are you offering?"

Eli shrugged. "I don't know yet. Depends on who offers us the best information."

The man groaned. Then finally said, "We were supposed to grab the woman with the baby."

Maggie's lungs deflated. The hallway darkened for a brief moment before she inhaled enough air to keep herself conscious.

She forced herself not to run screaming down the hall and kept her eyes trained on Reese, whose relaxed posture had disappeared. Tension radiated from him as his hands curled into fists at his side. "Why?"

The low word sent shivers down her spine. She could see the steel in his eyes from where she stood.

"I don't know why. We were just told to watch her then grab her and the kid. While we were watching, we noticed she went to the bank once a week. So we came up with the plan. The money from the bank was a bonus. But we had to make it look like a hostage situation."

"Then what?"

"Then we were to take her to an address."

"Where?" Eli demanded.

"An abandoned warehouse on the edge of town." He gave them the address. Maggie heard him say, "Now, you're going to give me a deal right? What kind of deal? I told you everything I know."

"You still haven't given us a name," Reese said. "Who's your boss?"

"I don't know, I never got a name. Just a contact number with a note in my mailbox saying if I wanted to make a lot of money to call it."

Eli snorted. "And of course you couldn't turn that down, could you?"

Silence echoed through the room for a moment and Maggie began to shake. She couldn't comprehend what she was hearing. Someone had paid to have her and Belle kidnapped. Under the guise of a fake bank robbery?

And if it hadn't been for Reese being in the right place at the right time, that someone would have succeeded.

She shook off the thought as one question took up residence at the forefront of her mind.

Who?

FIFTEEN

Reese paced the office and jammed his hands into his coat pockets. The police station heater was broken, and it was cold. He blew out, watching his breath form small clouds in front of his face. He shook his head and shivered.

Sitting at his desk netted him nothing and he thought about heading over to Maggie's and giving Cal a break. At least Maggie's house would be warm. Or maybe he'd go sit in his cruiser.

But he was waiting for a phone call.

He stood and walked into Eli's office. The man had a wool scarf wrapped around his neck, and he had his warm Sherpa coat buttoned up. A small space heater at his feet ran full blast. Eli looked up and Reese asked, "How'd you know about Patterson's dad's ranch?"

"His father finally called me back and said he hadn't seen his son since the night he and his buddies were over there. I took a shot in the dark."

"Good shot. Same with the money in the bank?"

Eli held up a report. "I got this from Spartanburg P.D. Alice scanned and emailed it to my phone right before we got to the hospital. They found an account number in Compton's apartment along with a brochure about Mexico. Another shot."

Reese smiled. "You're pretty good at that."

Eli shrugged. "It worked. Sometimes it does, sometimes it doesn't."

Reese changed the subject. "What do you know about Maggie's husband?"

Eli's eyes clouded as he leaned back in his chair to give Reese his full attention. "He wasn't a very nice man, and he was killed about seven months ago. Hit and run." The flat response said he knew more than he was letting on.

"I'm not asking you to betray a confidence. In fact, Maggie's told me most of it, I think. And I've been thinking about what she's told me."

"Tell me what you're thinking."

"All right." He hunched his shoulders and leaned forward. "Her husband was killed. The killer was never caught. We know that the bank robbery was a cover as an attempt to kidnap her and Belle. What if we need to do a little more digging into her husband's death?"

Eli was silent for a few moments and Reese held his tongue as he let the man think. Finally, his boss said, "You think it's all connected?"

"I don't know." Reese grimaced. "Might be a long shot."

"But it might not be a bad idea. I can't think of anything else that would have someone after her. What was he involved in? Did she tell you that?"

"No. I did a background check on him and it's pretty spotless. A couple of parking tickets, but nothing major. I don't know. I mean, it's just a thought. Probably a crazy one, but one I don't want to overlook and regret later."

Eli gave a slow nod. "Why don't you take that and run with it?"

Reese offered a small smile. "I'm waiting for a phone call now."

No sooner had the words left his lips than the phone on

his desk rang. He bolted from Eli's office and snatched it to his ear. "Kirkpatrick here."

"Hey, Reese. I think I've got what you're looking for." Colt Harris, a friend of his from Maggie's hometown of Spartanburg, South Carolina.

"What did you find out?"

"A lot. How much time do you have?"

Reese shivered and said, "Call me back on my cell." He rattled off the number, hung up and hollered to Eli. "I'm going to find someplace warm."

Eli's laugh drifted to him. "Don't blame you a bit."

As Reese exited the police station, his cell phone rang. He answered, "Go ahead. Fill me in."

"All right, first of all, it looks like your lady's in-laws have filed a custody suit."

Reese stopped dead in his tracks, ignoring the swirling white snow that had started to come down. "What? You're kidding!" Just what Maggie needed.

"Yep. While I was checking out your guy, Kent Bennett, I came across his folks and decided to see what they had to say about his death."

"And?"

"At first, I thought they were a cold couple. Showed no real emotion when I started questioning them. Then I mentioned Maggie and the baby and the woman starts weeping, saying she can't believe their son is gone and they're going to do everything they can to get their granddaughter."

Reese closed his eyes then clicked the remote to unlock his truck. He climbed in and slammed the door. Jamming the key into the ignition, he shivered. The engine caught and he reached over to turn the heat on full blast. As the cold air turned warm, he concentrated on the information Colt was sharing.

"It's been seven months. When did they start the process on all of this?"

"A couple of months ago, but no one seemed to be able to track Maggie down. She didn't have a credit card in her name until about a month ago. She uses cash for everything and she put all the utilities in her maiden name."

"She was hiding?" He hadn't gotten that impression.

"Looks like it."

"I'll ask her about that. What else?"

"Still working on the hit-and-run with Bennett."

"I told you about the witness that heard him arguing with someone that night. Did you track the witness down to question him again?"

"I did. Found him in the soup kitchen." Reese heard a page flip in Colt's notebook. "He described Bennett as angry, stomping up and down and flapping his hands like a 'chicken gone crazy' while the other person sat in the car and listened, then started screaming back at him."

"What about who Bennett was arguing with? Did you get a description?"

"Not a good one. I looked for any cameras that might have gotten everything on tape, but there weren't any on that block. But our witness says the person was smaller than Bennett, that he was wearing all black with a heavy overcoat and a black hat. The witness never got a look at the guy's face."

"Huh, of course. It's couldn't be that easy," Reese grunted. "I wonder whose idea it was to meet there then. Isolated, off the main road…could be more than a crime of opportunity. Maybe it was planned?"

"I know, I thought about that. But we won't know that answer until we catch this person Bennett met with. So anyway, the parents hired a P.I. to find Maggie and when she got her cell phone last month and that credit card, he found her. She should be getting a letter about the custody thing sometime this week."

"He was watching her credit."

"Yep."

"Why wait this long to contact her?" Reese rubbed a hand down the side of his cheek and turned the heater down a notch.

"They've been trying to build a case against her, I think. From what I can tell, they're saying she's an unfit mother."

Reese sat up in the seat. "On what grounds?"

"Based on an incident that happened in a store about two weeks after Belle was born."

"What happened?"

"Maggie apparently went shopping and left her baby unattended in an aisle. The sister-in-law happened to be in the store and watched the baby until Maggie came back to get her."

"I don't believe it," he stated flatly.

"Ask her about it. See what she says. I mean these people seemed nice enough once they warmed up to me and I think they really do want the baby. If the mother's not fit, I think they'd give Belle a good home."

Reese didn't speak for a moment as his mind raced with all the new information. "Well, she's fit. More than fit. I'm not really worried that they would win. But I hate for Maggie to have to go through the whole drama of them suing for custody." He paused and tapped the steering wheel. "Okay, keep me updated. See what you can find out about that green car. And check out where his family was the night he was killed."

"Will do."

Reese frowned as he hung up. He had to warn Maggie that her in-laws had filed for custody before she got the lawyer's letter.

* * *

Maggie walked into the den and dropped the mail onto the coffee table. Cal had played delivery man for her so she didn't have to walk to the mailbox. Frankly, she could use a little fresh air, but it wasn't worth risking if someone was still after her. And Reese seemed to think someone was.

Shannon had taken Belle grocery shopping for their Thanksgiving dinner. Shannon said Maggie needed some time for herself and besides, Maggie really should stay put and not put anyone in danger by leaving the house and having someone try to kill her again.

"Thanks bunches, Shannon," Maggie muttered as she paced from one end of the den to the other. But she couldn't deny the truth in the woman's words, so she'd relented.

As a result, Maggie had finished her classes, had one Individualized Education Plan meeting on a student and written another IEP for the meeting that would be held first thing Monday morning. Working with special education high school students was a challenge that fulfilled her in a way she'd never dreamed possible.

But it involved a lot of paperwork. While she'd worked on that, she'd managed to push thoughts of being a target out of her mind.

Now, as she paced, she thought. Was Reese right? Did Kent's death have something to do with everything that was happening now? The bank robbery was a setup. She and Belle were supposed to be kidnapped.

And then what?

Why?

They were supposed to deliver them to an address. What had Reese found out about that location? Who could be behind such a horrible thing?

She let out a groan, dropped to her knees and let her chin fall to her chest. "Father, I don't know what to do now. I pray You're working behind the scenes here because I'm lost and floundering and I'm so tired. Please help us."

A tear slid down her cheek, but her heart felt lighter. As if some of the burden had been lifted from her shoulders.

The presence of God. Her troubles and worries weren't magically gone, but she had help. She didn't have to do this alone. Maggie drew in a deep breath. "Thank You," she whispered.

God never promised that life would be easy for those who chose to trust Him, but He did promise to walk through the hard times with them.

And she was certainly going through a hard time.

The doorbell rang and she rose to walk into the foyer. Peeking through the window, she smiled.

Another thing she had to give God the credit for.

He'd sent Reese into her life just when she needed him.

She opened the door with a smile. "Hi."

"Hi."

The serious look on his face sent her smile into a nosedive. "What is it?" Snow drifted down in a gentle veil of white outside as he stepped inside and shrugged out his coat. "Oh, goodness, I didn't realize it was snowing so much. I'm going to call Shannon and ask her to get on back here before the roads get bad."

He nodded. "Good idea. Then we need to talk."

"All right."

She led him into the den then picked up the phone to dial Shannon. Reese settled himself on the couch while Maggie listened to the phone ring. When it went to voice mail, she frowned, but said, "Shannon, it's snowing pretty hard out there. Why don't you go ahead and bring Belle on home. I'm a little worried about your getting stuck on the road. Call me as soon as you get this." She hung up and looked at Reese. "Hopefully, she'll call me back soon. Or see the snow and realize she needs to get home." Maggie took a deep breath to settle her nerves. Belle and Shannon would be fine. But she sent up a silent prayer for their safety. "Okay, so what has you looking like you have bad news?"

"I had a conversation with a buddy of mine who lives in Spartanburg."

"Okay."

"After all the crazy stuff going on around here, I asked him to look into a few things."

"Kent's hit-and-run?"

"Right."

Maggie rubbed her suddenly sweaty palms on her jean-clad thighs. "And?"

He blew out a breath. "There's no easy way to say this."

"You're scaring me, Reese."

"Your in-laws plan to sue you for custody of Belle by proving that you're an unfit mother. The letter's on the way—if you haven't already gotten it."

The bottom dropped out of her stomach. Stunned, she simply looked at him. Then she shot to her feet and grabbed the mail from the coffee table. One by one, she went through the envelopes, tossing them aside. Until she came across one that said Billings and Jordan, Attorneys at Law.

Maggie ripped the envelope open, read through the information that Reese had just delivered. She tossed the paper onto the table and shook her head. "How can they do this?" She paced to the mantel then back. "They can't take her away from me. I won't let them."

Reese stood and placed his hands on her shoulders. "Calm down a second. I said they were suing. I didn't say they'd win."

She paused and looked up at him. Tears hovered on the edges of her lashes, but she refused to let them fall. "I'll fight them," she whispered. "Every step of the way, no matter what I have to do or how much it costs. I have money, Reese, a lot of money that my grandfather left me. They will *not* have her."

He blinked at her statement about the money, but addressed her last comment. "I don't think they have any grounds. They'd have to prove that you're an unfit mother. An investigation would be carried out and once they realized there's no evidence, they wouldn't have a case."

At his reassuring and confident words, Maggie felt herself start to relax a fraction. "But they could still cause us a lot of grief."

"Unfortunately, yes. They could."

"They've never seen her, Reese. Not even once. They didn't come to the hospital, they never called, they don't know who she is or—"

He placed a finger over her lips. "I know. I really don't think you have anything to worry about." He gave a tug on her shoulders and she slipped into his arms to rest her head on his chest. She felt him place a kiss on the top of her head. Maggie closed her eyes and allowed peace to wash over her for just a moment. So this was what it felt like to be loved, to be cared for by a man who didn't feel the need to control and hurt.

But she'd thought Kent was this way in the beginning, too. She tensed and moved away. Reese let her go without protest, but the question in his eyes hurt.

He cleared his throat. "I'm fall—" He stopped and shoved his hands in his pockets. "I care about you a lot, Maggie. More than a lot. I want us to see if we have a chance at a relationship. I want to see if we maybe have a future together."

The words hit her like a punch to the gut. "Oh, Reese."

"You don't have to say anything right now. Just think about it."

She wanted to yell, "I have thought about it." But didn't. Because she still had doubts about her ability to make a sound judgment when it came to men.

Kent would have demanded an immediate answer. And if it wasn't the one he liked, he would have pouted and sulked or simply beat her until she gave in. No, Reese wasn't anything like Kent. Even by comparing them, she was insulting Reese. And in that instant, she knew Reese would never raise a hand to her. They might fight and argue, even raise their voices to one another. But he'd never hit her—or hurt her on purpose.

Maggie stepped forward and wrapped her arms around his neck and brought his lips to hers. After a long, sweet moment, his surprise melted into a tender response. When they parted, she smiled at him. "I care about you, too, Reese."

He gave a relieved laugh. "Good."

She glanced at the clock then at the phone. Her smile flipped into a frown. "I'm worried."

He walked to the window and looked out. "It looks like the snow is slowing down, but the temperature's hovering around freezing. Shannon probably should be on her way back."

Maggie dialed Shannon's number again. When Shannon still didn't pick up, Maggie swallowed hard. "I don't like this."

"Wait a minute." He cocked his head to the right. "Call it again."

She frowned, but pressed the redial button. And then she heard what he did. She walked down the hall, the faint sound growing louder with each step. By the time they reached Maggie's bedroom, the ringing continued then stopped.

Maggie walked into her room and saw Shannon's overnight bag beside the bed, packed in a haphazard fashion. Shannon's cell phone lay on the end table. But it wasn't the phone that captured her attention, it was the large manilla envelope sticking out of Shannon's bag.

Her grandfather's name was on the return address portion. And she had seen this envelope before. She reached out with only a twinge of guilt about invading her sister-in-law's privacy, pulled the envelope from the bag.

"What is it?" Reese asked.

A bad feeling churned in her gut. "It's the information my grandfather sent me," she whispered. "After we got in touch and I said I wanted to visit, he sent me all this information on Rose Mountain, this house, everything about his will and what to do when he died. Everything." She swallowed hard. "He said he sent it, but I never received the first package. So he sent a second one. We just assumed the first one got lost in the mail. Unless—" She rose and hurried past Reese and into her office. She dropped the package she'd found in Shannon's bag onto the floor and fell to her knees. She opened the small file cabinet beside her desk. Maggie reached in and pulled out a matching manilla envelope. She looked up at Reese. "He sent the first package about three months before I was due with Belle. When it didn't come, he sent another one." She bit her lip, worry and that bad feeling in her stomach gnawing away at her. "Why would Shannon have this first package?"

A frown drew his brows together over his nose. "I don't know. Maybe she found it in Kent's things and decided to give it to you. Because it's highly likely that your husband got to the mail first and took it."

"I thought about that," she said, "but when he didn't

confront me with it, I figured it had gotten lost after all."
She paused. "And if Shannon found it, why hasn't she
given it to me yet?"

"Good question." He shrugged. "Maybe she forgot."

"Maybe." She glanced at the clock again and a pang of
fear shot through her. "Reese, I'm getting scared that Shannon and Belle aren't back yet."

He nodded. "Let me put a BOLO out on her car and
see if I get some answers." He walked to the window and
looked out. "At least it's not snowing anymore."

"But the roads are wet, and it's a little below freezing.
That's not good."

His phone rang and he snatched it, listened for a moment then paled. "I've got to go. There's been an accident
just outside of town. I'm a first responder. They may need
my skills before an ambulance can get out there."

Her knees went week. "It's not Shannon's car is it?"

"No, a black Ford Taurus. Jason's going to be here and
will keep a watch on you. I'll be looking for Shannon on
my way out to the accident. If I see her, or if I get a report
of anyone else seeing her, I'll call or text you."

Maggie nodded. "All right. They're probably fine.
Maybe she got to talking to someone in the grocery store."

"Maybe."

Maggie walked with him to the front door and saw him
jog to the cruiser still sitting in the driveway. He spoke to
Jason who nodded then, with a wave in her direction, Reese
climbed into his own cruiser and left.

She ached at his absence. Having him around made her
feel safe. Confident that things would work out. When he
left, he took that feeling with him.

"Which is why I don't need to rely on my feelings,
right, God? That's why I need to trust in You. In Your con-
stant and abiding promise to be with me no matter what.

Lord, please watch over Belle and Shannon. Bring them safely home," she whispered. Saying the words helped, even though the worry lingered.

For the next thirty minutes, she paced the floor. No word from Shannon, nothing from Reese.

The phone rang and Maggie jerked. She didn't recognize the number, but snatched her handset from the coffee table. "Hello?"

"Oh, Maggie, I'm so glad I got you."

"Shannon! Where are you? Is Belle all right?"

"Yes, we're fine."

Maggie's pulse slowed. She walked to the window to look out, half expecting to see Shannon driving up the drive. "Where have you been? I expected you an hour and a half ago." She sighed. "And now it's snowing again."

"I know. But don't worry, we're fine. We're just stuck."

"Stuck? Stuck where?"

"Near a little country store. I left my cell phone at the house so I had to walk a little ways to find this pay phone."

"Is Belle warm enough?"

"Of course she is," Shannon snapped. "I know how to take care of her."

Maggie blinked at the woman's sharp tone. Then Shannon said, "Sorry, sorry. I didn't mean to be crabby. It's been a rough couple of hours with the snow, the cold and the car that quit on me."

"Of course," Maggie soothed. "Don't worry. I'll come get you. Give me directions."

Maggie listened as Shannon described how to find her. For someone who didn't know the town very well, Shannon gave her pretty good directions. Maggie had never been where Shannon directed her, but thought she could find it easily enough.

"I'll be there as fast as I can."

Before she left, she sent a text to Reese to let him know Shannon and Belle had been found and were safe. She waved to Jason. "I need to go somewhere. You want to follow me or drive?"

His eyes went wide. "Hop in."

SIXTEEN

Reese placed a call to his buddy in Spartanburg and got him working on a hunch. The faster he got some answers to the questions running through his head, the better off they'd all be.

He arrived at the scene of the accident and winced when he saw the family of four sitting off to the side of the road. Mom, Dad and two kids. A boy about six and a little girl who looked to be around nine. They looked cold and miserable, but otherwise not seriously injured.

EMTs hadn't arrived yet. Eli had a first aid kit out and was patching up a nasty-looking cut over the little girl's eye. Reese grabbed a handful of blankets he always kept in the truck for emergencies.

Cal drove up and Dr. Dylan Seabrook got out of the cruiser.

"Paul, Stacy, are you guys all right? What happened?" Dylan hurried toward the shaken family.

Cal looked at Eli. "I figured it wouldn't hurt to pick him up on my way out here."

Eli nodded. "Good idea."

Reese helped Dylan wrap the blankets around the shivering family and escort them to sit in the warm cruiser. Then he looked at the black Ford Taurus kissing the large oak tree on the side of the road. He leaned into the cruiser and looked at the man Dylan had called Paul. "What happened?"

A shock of red hair fell over the man's forehead. His blue eyes narrowed, his brow furrowed as he spoke. "I was just telling Eli that this car came out of nowhere and ran us off the road."

Reese pulled his green notebook from his front pocket, ignoring the blast of wind trying to sneak down the back of his heavy coat. "Someone in a hurry?"

"Must have been."

"No," his wife said from the backseat. "It was deliberate. Someone ran us off the road on purpose."

Reese lifted a brow. A three-way stop lay just ahead in the direction the family had been traveling. Another side road connected to the main road about fifty yards from the intersection. "Looks like the car that hit you was coming out of that side road, you rounded the corner and got slammed."

"That's exactly what happened," Paul said. "But I don't think it was deliberate."

Stacy's expression said she disagreed.

Reese noticed that Cal had the little boy in his arms, wrapped in a blanket and was walking him over to join his parents and sister in the car. The child appeared unhurt, just scared. But he seemed willing to be entertained by Cal's badge.

Reese walked to the damaged Taurus. The front hood had crumpled up and now rested against the spiderwebbed windshield.

He checked the side that had been hit. Ran his fingers along the dented metal. He returned to the cruiser. Paul held his son in his lap now. One of the father's arms dangled, useless, to rest on the seat. Pain drew the man's brows down and a muscle ticked in his jaw. His good hand held his son against his chest. Reese asked, "Do you know what kind of car hit you?"

Paul shook his head. "No, sorry. I just had a flash of something coming toward me, then we hit the tree."

The little girl looked at him, opened her mouth to say something then closed it. Reese moved to her side of the car to look past Stacy and focus his attention on the child. "What's your name, sweetheart?" Her blue eyes looked extra large under the white bandage now covering the gash in her forehead. She moved closer to her mother, but didn't take her gaze from him. Reese tried again. "Can you tell me what you saw?"

Stacy wrapped an arm around her daughter's shoulder. "Lisa, if you saw the car, will you tell the deputy what it looked like?"

"It was white," she said then pulled the blanket up over her lips and nose. Her eyes stayed on him.

Reese smiled at the girl. "Thanks, Lisa, that helps. Was it a truck like mine or a car like yours?"

"It was just a car."

"It was a Mercedes," the little boy stated.

Reese lifted a brow. "It was?" He looked at the boy's father. "Would he know that?"

Paul nodded. "Yeah. He knows all the car symbols. I travel a lot and we make a game out of it when he comes with me. The person who spots the most Beemers wins a milk shake. Then we do Toyotas or Mercedes or Fords. Then we both get milk shakes." He shrugged, winced and went pale.

Dylan, who had walked up to peer into the cruiser, grunted. "Keep that shoulder still, Paul. I'm pretty sure it's dislocated." He looked at the shaken family. "Good thing you all had your seat belts on."

Sirens sounded to his left and Reese looked up to see two ambulances barreling toward them. They'd come from Bryson City.

Then his mind went back to what Paul's son said. Cold dread settled in his gut. Shannon drove a white Mercedes. Of course there was more than one white Mercedes in the state, but...

"Eli, how many people around here drive that kind of car?"

Eli met his gaze. "I can only think of one."

Reese blew out a breath and nodded. "I was afraid of that." He rubbed his gloved hand against his thigh. "I already have an unofficial BOLO out on her because she's got Belle, and Maggie was getting worried." Small towns did that kind of thing. Just one more thing Reese liked about Rose Mountain.

"Yeah, I heard that," Eli said. He pulled out his radio. "Well, now it's official. If it wasn't her, at least we can rule her out."

Reese's phone buzzed.

His buddy from Spartanburg. "Trevor, what do you have?"

"Nothing yet on that pill you sent, but it's coming."

"Then what?"

"You know how you're always saying go with your gut?"

"Yeah."

"I did and it paid off."

Excitement began to hum in Reese's veins. "Tell me."

"Everything you've told me about what's going on with your lady friend had me suspicious. Especially after you sent that pill in the aspirin bottle and Maggie said it must belong to her sister-in-law."

Reese frowned. "All right. And?"

"And so I started looking into the night Maggie's husband was killed. You may already know some of this, but here's what I got. First of all, the witness wasn't reliable. A homeless guy who saw two people arguing. After checking out Kent Bennett's background, it came to light that he was deeply in debt."

"To whom?"

"To some pretty nasty characters."

"Right. So it's safe to assume that he was probably killed by one of them?"

"That would be the first assumption. I decided to keep looking. And when I got to his family, things turned real interesting."

"How?" He wished the man would just hurry up and spit it out.

"Turns out the nasty characters didn't do the killing." Reese didn't even want to know how Trevor could be certain of that. He knew his buddy had contacts better left under their rocks. Reese had been in that territory a few times in his career and he never cared to go back. Trevor said, "They were furious the man was dead."

"Because they'd never get their money, right?"

"Right."

"So if they didn't kill him, who did?"

"Someone driving a green car. The paint chips the ME found embedded in Mr. Bennett's clothing told us that much."

"But you have something up your sleeve. What is it you're not telling me?"

"Because of my highly suspicious nature, I decided to check into whether anyone in the family had a green car. No one did."

"What about—"

"A rental. Yeah, I thought about that. And I hit pay dirt."

"Who?"

"A woman by the name of Shannon Bennett rented a green BMW from the airport the night her brother was killed."

Chills that had nothing to do with the cold weather raced up his spine. "Anything else?"

"Nope. I'll let you know when the report comes back on the pill."

"Thanks."

No sooner had he hung up than the phone buzzed again. A text from Maggie.

SHANNON CALLED. HER CAR BROKE DOWN. ON THE WAY TO MEET HER AT SIMON'S STOP AND GO. JASON IS WITH ME.

He looked up. "Hey, Eli. Just got a text from Maggie. She said she was on the way to meet Shannon. Her car broke down."

"Where?"

"Simon's Stop and Go."

Reese frowned. Why did that sound familiar.

Eli's head snapped up and Reese saw a flash of worry darken his eyes. "What is it?"

Reese said, "That's the place where Maggie and Belle were supposed to be delivered after the bank robbery."

Maggie squinted through the still-falling snow. At least it wasn't too heavy. Hopefully, she would have Belle and Shannon back home safe and sound before too long, and then it could snow all it wanted.

Jason slowed the cruiser, his head nodding to the right. "Should be right around here. I come out this way every once in a while, but not often."

"There aren't any lights on. Is it closed?"

"Probably. Around here businesses close up if it's snowing and dropping to the freezing mark. No one wants to try to get home on icy roads."

"Right."

She bit her lip and glanced up at the sun. In an hour it would be gone. And the temperatures would drop fast. But she was here now and in an hour would be home.

Nothing to worry about.

Except the place looked deserted. "Where are they?" Maggie wondered as she climbed from the vehicle.

Jason got out and glanced around the area. "Kind of creepy, isn't it?"

Maggie shot him a perturbed look. "Well, I didn't think so until you pointed it out." He gave her a sheepish smile and hitched his pants up as he walked toward the front door. Maggie followed him, uneasiness making her skin ripple. "Shannon? We're here." Where was she? Why hadn't she met them at the door? Had someone else come along and rescued her and Belle?

Confusion and a renewed anxiety to see Belle overshadowed her skittish nerves and Maggie rushed through the door after Deputy White.

She could see him standing in the middle of the store looking around. "Ms. Bennett?"

A loud pop sounded.

Maggie flinched and spun toward the sound. A second passed before she realized Jason had been shot. Surprise settled on his face and he lifted a hand to cover the rapidly spreading red stain on his chest.

SEVENTEEN

The minute Eli finished his statement, Reese was headed for his cruiser. Eli was right behind him in his own car. Over the radio, Eli told him, "I'm getting Cal and Mitchell for backup. I don't like this any more than you do."

Reese cranked the car and let Eli pull out first. Eli knew the fastest route to the place. With one hand on the wheel, he dialed Maggie's number. A number he'd programmed into his phone. Speed dial number one.

He held the phone to his ear and listened to it ring. "Come on, Maggie, pick up."

Her phone went to voice mail.

Reese hung up, and his worry meter shot off the chart. She'd just texted him thirty minutes ago. Why wasn't she answering?

Eli made a left, then a right, then they were on the main road going toward the edge of town. Reese wanted to floor it, but there were too many side roads, the sun was sinking behind the mountain to his right and he didn't want to take a chance on hitting someone who may decide not to come to a complete stop at the numerous stop signs lining the road.

So he gritted his teeth and kept it ten miles over the speed limit.

* * *

"Jason!" Maggie screamed as she raced to the fallen deputy's side. She dropped to her knees beside the man and felt for a pulse. She looked up and saw Shannon standing in the doorway that looked like it might lead back into a pantry. "Get down!" Maggie yelled. "Someone's shooting!" Then Maggie noticed the gun in the woman's hand and froze. "You?" she whispered.

"Me." She lifted the weapon and Maggie screamed and ducked, rolling toward the counter, searching for any kind of cover she could find. The bullet shattered the glass display behind her.

"Stop! What are you doing? Why?" Maggie felt the terror choke her, closing her throat, numbing her reflexes, freezing her brain. "Shannon, stop! Talk to me!"

"He promised me the baby." The flat monotone spiked Maggie's fear. Horror flooded her as she tried to piece together what Shannon was saying.

"What baby? Who promised you a baby?"

"Kent. He promised to give me the baby when she was born."

Realization dawned. "What? Give you my baby? Are you crazy?"

"Actually, yes. At least that's what the doctors tell me." Shannon moved and Maggie could see her in the round mirror above the door. Shannon held the weapon like she knew how to use it. But then she'd already taken Jason down with no trouble. The deputy lay still, pale as death. Maggie wanted to go to him. Help him, but knew if she moved Shannon would shoot her.

She licked her lips. "Where's Belle?"

"Belle's fine. Don't worry about Belle. Belle's mine now. I'm going to take care of her like I should have all along."

"Why did he promise you Belle, Shannon? You should know I'd never give up my baby."

"You were negligent! I proved that in the store."

Maggie knew immediately what the woman referred to. She'd been desperate to get out of the house. So, when Belle was about three weeks old, Maggie had strolled her up to the shopping center. In one of the stores, Maggie had turned to look at something and when she turned back, Belle was gone. "You took her."

"I wanted to teach you a lesson. Show you that you couldn't take care of her."

"You scared me to death."

"We were one aisle over. You should have realized that you were in no shape to take care of her."

"She's mine!"

"No, she's mine." It wasn't the words that sent sheer fear shuddering through her, it was the without-a-doubt certainty with which Shannon said the words that scared her senseless.

"Why did he promise to give her to you? Why?" Shannon knew her husband hadn't wanted the baby, but to think he'd schemed to get rid of her...

"I can't have children, and I can't adopt. Belle was my one hope to be a mother." Shannon's voice cracked, then steadied. "And I *will* be her mother. He was going to give her to me. Then he took her away." She paused. "He took her away!"

Maggie flinched. "So you killed him." Somehow she knew it. She didn't know why, she just knew it was true.

A perfectly arched brow lifted over one cold eye. "I did. He found the envelope your grandfather sent you. He came home early that day and found it in the mailbox. When he looked inside, he knew your baby was going to rescue him from the gambling debts he'd managed to rack up. If you were dead, the money would go to whoever got custody of Belle."

Maggie's breaths came in pants. She had to get out of here. Had to do something to save herself. Save Belle. But Belle wasn't here.

She froze as something warm touched the back of her neck. Shannon's voice hissed in her ear. "Now it'll be my money. And Belle will be mine, too."

"Not without my signature," Maggie blurted out.

The woman behind her froze. "What do you mean?"

"I changed the will. I changed everything. Unless you have my signature on a new will, my death means nothing."

"You're lying." But Maggie could hear a faint thread of worry in her voice.

"Then kill me and find out," Maggie bluffed, keeping her words low and steady.

A slight pause. "Go."

"What?"

"In the car. Go."

Maggie stood on trembling legs, using the counter to pull herself up. The gun jabbed her lower back and she stumbled out from behind the counter. Her gaze fell to Jason, bleeding on the floor. Maggie moved toward him. "Let me help him."

"No." Shannon shoved her once again and Maggie tripped over Jason, landing with a thud half on top of him, half on the floor. His weapon still in his holster, her fingers closed over the butt.

"Get up!" Shannon screamed. "I'm sure you told someone you were coming here! Now move! Into the police car."

Maggie pulled on the gun. But it wouldn't move, still strapped into the holster. And she didn't have time to figure out how to release it. "I'm sorry, Jason," she whispered. But she'd had no idea that Shannon was so unstable.

"Let's go now!"

Maggie thought fast. "I need the keys. They're in his pocket."

"Then hurry up and get them!" Shannon screamed at her. Maggie dug into the pocket with her right hand, hoping Shannon wasn't paying attention to her left.

Maggie got the keys, stood, stumbled and got her balance. She shoved her hands into her pockets and made her way to the door. "Take me to Belle, Shannon."

"Not a chance. Into the driver's seat."

Maggie stepped out into the cold, the wind biting at her bare face. She made her way through the swirling snow, got to the car, opened the door and slid behind the wheel.

She pulled the keys from her right pocket and jammed them into the ignition. "Where am I going?"

"To get the paper you need to sign so that I get Belle and all the money."

Maggie swallowed hard. "It's at my house."

Shannon simply glared at her, the gun never wavering. "Then go home."

Reese pulled into the parking lot of Simon's Stop and Go and stared at the dark building. His heart sank. He didn't have to examine the structure to know they weren't there.

Eli sidled up beside him. Cal and Mitchell turned in, too. Reese opened the door and raced toward the store, leaving the car running, the car door open.

He pushed the unlocked door open and stepped inside. His eyes landed on Jason. "Oh, no."

Reese launched himself to the deputy's side and felt for a pulse. Faint and weak, but there.

As he was reaching for his radio to call for help, Eli and the other officer came through the door. When Eli saw Jason on the floor, he gave a harsh exclamation and dropped to the floor opposite Reese. "Is he alive?"

"Barely." Speaking into the radio, he gave their location. "Officer down, send a helicopter." He looked at Eli. "It can land in the parking lot."

"Absolutely."

He spotted something on the floor near the counter and got to his feet. He reached down and picked up a scarf. "It's Maggie's. She was here."

Eli still had his finger on Jason's pulse. He looked up and nodded. "I'll get Mitchell to stay with Jason. The rest of us need to figure out where Maggie and Shannon went. His keys are missing and his cruiser's gone."

Reese nodded. "They're in his car. You got a GPS tracker on that thing?"

"Yeah." While Eli called that in, Reese gave the store another once-over, but didn't see anything else that might give him a clue as to where Maggie might be going.

"His radio's gone."

"What?"

Eli looked up. "Jason's radio. It's missing."

Reese frowned and wondered what that meant.

He turned his up and listened.

Nothing but police chatter about the nightmare he was living. "I'll keep listening. Someone took that radio for a purpose. If he—or she—wants to get in touch with one of us, we need to be paying attention."

"Good idea. I'm just going to—"

Reese cut him off with a wave as he lifted the radio to his hear. Maggie was saying, "...knows I'm with you, Shannon, he'll know you're involved in this."

"You're lying. Now shut up and drive."

Reese looked at Eli. "Maggie has it."

* * *

With her left hand in her pocket, holding down the button to transmit, she drove with her right hand. She'd managed to turn the volume all the way down on the radio so Shannon wouldn't be able to hear any transmissions coming through, but if there was someone listening, they'd hear her and Shannon talking.

Please God, let there be someone listening.

"Tell me why you killed Kent. He was your brother."

"He was a liar," Shannon snarled, spittle flying from her tense lips.

"But to kill him…" Maggie bit her lip. "Did you plan it all along?"

"No, of course not. It was something we planned together. I wanted a baby. He didn't want 'the brat.'" Maggie glanced out the corner of her eye and saw Shannon frown in disgust. "To call that beautiful baby a brat was awful. *Kent* was awful. I begged him to let me have her, and he agreed."

"But why? There had to be something in it for him."

"He got to keep you," she said with a shrug.

Maggie flinched. She never would have survived living with Kent if he'd given Belle away. And she never would have seen her baby again if Shannon had had her way.

And now she was in the same situation. Unless she got Shannon to give up, she'd never hold Belle again. The thought was enough to freeze her muscles. Maggie swallowed hard and focused on driving.

"He found that letter from your grandfather. He was planning to kill you—did you know that?" Shannon said it conversationally, as though her words didn't hold the power of a boxer's punch.

"What?" Maggie gaped long enough to run off the road

onto the edge. Tires crunched and the wheel jerked from her grasp.

Shannon screamed and waved her weapon. "Pay attention!"

Maggie got control of the car. "How do you know that? I thought you just said he planned to give you Belle and keep me. Why would he want to kill me?"

"For the money. That's why he had to die."

"Money?" Maggie blinked. "I'm confused."

Shannon gave a long-suffering sigh. "You haven't put it together yet? He found the envelope in the mail after he promised me Belle."

The envelope. Realization dawned. "And once he saw that Belle came with the money only upon my death, he knew he had to keep her and get rid of me," Maggie whispered.

"Exactly."

"So he backed out of your agreement."

"And I threatened to tell you." Shannon shook her head. "Two weeks before I killed him, he tried to kill me, can you believe it? He grabbed me around the throat and..." She gulped and shuddered. "I got away from him, but knew it wouldn't be the last time he tried. I knew I had to get rid of him."

"So you hit him with a car?"

"I did." A hard, determined expression crossed Shannon's face. A look so scary that Maggie winced. "The opportunity just was suddenly there and without even really thinking, I just...did it. I pressed the gas pedal and..." A slight smile curved her lips. "I did it and it was so easy." The smile disappeared and she gave Maggie a bitter look. "I knew I was in your will to be guardian of Belle if something happened to you and Kent. Well, something happened to Kent. Now it's your turn."

The woman was sick, mentally ill. Maggie whispered, "You really think you'll get away with killing me, too?"

"After you sign that paper, I will."

"They're going to Maggie's house," Reese said over the radio to Eli. "Shannon killed her brother and it looks like she plans to kill Maggie." He shuddered at the information he'd just overheard.

His phone buzzed, and he glanced at it. A text message from Trevor, his buddy in Spartanburg.

Eli took the next turn. "Is Belle with them?"

"No. Doesn't sound like it. Keep listening."

As they drove, Reese prayed. He snatched his phone and read the text.

And felt dread center itself in his gut. With a whispered prayer, he tossed the phone onto the passenger seat and grabbed his radio once again.

He knew Eli had called for backup from Bryson City, even Asheville, but that didn't mean they'd get there in time. "Eli, I don't know how volatile Shannon is. I found an aspirin bottle in Maggie's cabinet, only it wasn't aspirin in the bottle. I sent a pill to Asheville to be tested and it's medication used for people with schizophrenia."

A low whistle came through the radio as Eli processed what that might mean.

"But there are other reasons someone takes that kind of drug. Schizophrenia's just one of them." Reese said the words, but his gut didn't believe Shannon was taking the medication for anything else. If Shannon was truly mentally ill, Maggie had a whole different set of problems on her hands. And even if Shannon wasn't having a schizophrenic episode, she still had a gun and planned to get rid of Maggie. The only plus would be Shannon might be in a frame of mind to be reasoned with.

Maybe. Hopefully. His heart shuddered at the thought of Maggie being in a hostage situation. A SWAT team from Asheville was already en route.

Then again, if he and Eli got to Maggie's house in time, they could just stop Shannon in her tracks and be done with it. He liked that plan.

EIGHTEEN

Maggie pulled into her driveway and shut off the car, wishing she had a switch for the terror racing through her.

Shannon nudged her with the gun. "Now get out. And remember, I've got Belle."

"I don't need a reminder." Maggie released the radio in her left hand and opened the car door. Her mind spun as she tried to figure out what she was going to do. How she was going to get away and alert Reese. She prayed he was listening in and was on his way to her house, but she couldn't count on that.

What was she going to do? What about the will? A cold shudder ripped through her. She'd never mailed the envelope. The envelope containing the new will. If Maggie died now and Shannon got away with it, she would get custody of Belle.

"Inside." Shannon gave her a shove toward the door. Maggie walked, but her mind spun.

"This was all supposed to be taken care of before now," Shannon said. "I wasn't even supposed to be here. You were never supposed to see me." The pout in her voice scared Maggie. The woman sounded put out that she was being so inconvenienced. Maggie opened the door and stepped inside. She disabled the alarm and sent prayers heavenward. Shannon still muttered, waving the gun. Maggie slipped her hand in her pocket and pressed the button while Shannon continued her rant. "Those idiots I hired couldn't even follow a simple plan. Rob the bank, grab you and Belle and get out."

"And then what, Shannon? Kill me?"

"Yes. Exactly."

The flat statement in the annoyed tone made Maggie gulp. How could the woman talk about killing her as though she were just squashing a bug in her house?

Fear made her nauseous.

She had to hold it together. Think. Think. Where could Belle be? The only thing that kept Maggie from screaming the house down was the fact that she felt certain Shannon wouldn't hurt Belle.

"Where is it?"

The barrel of the gun kissed her lower back.

Her knees threatened to buckle.

She locked them and forced herself to walk toward her office.

Reese got on the radio to Eli. "Don't pull in the driveway. Stop before you get to her house. I want to case the place and see if I can possibly go in unarmed, pretend like I don't know anything is wrong."

The radio crackled then Eli asked, "You think that's a good idea? From what you've said, that woman is unstable."

"Right now, it's the best thing to do."

He rolled his car to a stop where the gravel began its crawl to Maggie's house. Eli pulled up behind him. He looked at Eli. "Keep your radio on."

"I'm right behind you."

Reese took off his heavy coat, but left his gloves on for now. He needed to be able to move easily, unencumbered by the heavy material of the Sherpa coat. But he needed his hand warm in case he had to use his weapon. Cold fingers were slow fingers. Once he got a look at the house, he'd decide whether or not to pull his glove off his right hand.

The gravel crunched under his feet. His eyes scanned the driveway, the house, the woods beyond. He could hear the water lapping against the dock in a silent soothing rhythm.

Jason's cruiser sat in the driveway. They were here. His heart thumped in a mix of anticipation of getting Maggie away from the woman and terror that he wouldn't be able to do so.

Eli's footfalls echoed behind him. Reese called Maggie's cell phone once again. And again, it went to voice mail.

He looked at Eli. "What's Shannon's number?"

Eli shook his head. "I have no idea, I'll get Alice to get it ASAP." He pressed the earpiece further into his ear and Reese knew he was listening to the sounds coming from Jason's radio. "Sounds like they're at the back of the house. Maybe in her office?"

Reese crept to the front of the house, then rounded the corner to the office window. She had the curtains pulled but if he peered in at the corner… There.

He had a perfect glimpse of the gun in Shannon's left hand.

Maggie's hands shook as she pretended to go through the files. "I had it in here."

"Why did you change it?"

Maggie paused and looked up, past the barrel of the gun into Shannon's mad, snapping eyes. "Because I just wasn't sure about you. And then you were here, living in my house, taking care of Belle and I thought…"

"What?" The gun lowered a fraction.

"I thought that you really loved Belle. That maybe I was wrong to change the will."

Confusion flickered through the madness. "Of course I love Belle. She's my only chance... Mom said that..."

"Your chance at what, Shannon?"

"Motherhood." Her jaw tightened and the confusion fled. So did the madness. Sanity now stared at Maggie as Shannon went on. "I had an abortion when I was twenty-four. A back-alley type thing that led to a hysterectomy when I didn't stop bleeding. I've been diagnosed with a mental illness, too, so adoption is out of the question." She snorted. "It's so unfair. As long as I take my medication, I'm fine."

Medication. The strange pills in the aspirin bottle that Reese had almost taken?

"So you decided to make Belle yours."

"From the minute I found out you were pregnant." She waved the gun. "Now get the paper."

But Maggie didn't move. "That's why you were so nice to me," she whispered. "You wanted my trust. You wanted me to think you were on my side and that you would help me..."

"And it was working just fine until Kent showed up and scared you off."

"I thought he would hurt you if I stayed." She remembered how Shannon had begged her not to leave, said she wasn't scared of Kent and didn't care what he thought about Maggie staying there. But Maggie had cared. Maggie had wanted to protect the woman from the violence that followed Kent wherever he went. Especially if he was displeased with someone. And he'd been very displeased with Maggie.

Shannon's grip tightened on the weapon. "I know. I was furious with him. All he had to do was stay away and..."

She broke off and screamed, "Now get the paper! I don't have time for this. They're probably looking for you right now."

Maggie could only pray that was so. She'd had to release the radio button to search the file box. It would have been too obvious if she'd left her hand in her pocket. However, she managed to snag the envelope addressed to the lawyer with the new will in it. With subtle ease, she maneuvered it into her pocket with the radio. "Tell me where Belle is, Shannon. I need to know where my baby is."

"She's safe. And she'll be with us. That's all you need to know."

"Us?" Before Shannon could answer, Maggie bent back over the file drawer and in one smooth move, snagged the horse-head paperweight in her right hand and brought it around to catch Shannon in left shoulder.

The woman screamed and dropped the gun. Maggie kicked it under the bed and bolted for the door.

Reese watched Shannon fall back against the wall as he threw himself through the window. Glass shattered around him, his back stung and his neck felt like someone had drawn a razor blade across it, but none of that mattered as Shannon's back disappeared through the doorway. "Now!" he yelled into the microphone.

The crash of the front door greeted his order.

"Shannon! It's the police! Drop your weapon!" He hollered the words, but didn't hold out hope they'd have any effect on the woman.

Scrambling to his feet, he bolted from the room.

He raced into the den and came up short. Shannon had managed to snag Maggie's blond ponytail and now had her at gunpoint in front of the fireplace.

Eli and Cal stood, weapons drawn.

A standoff.

Heart in his throat, Reese watched Shannon's eyes, looking for sanity. His stomach dropped as he saw the trapped look of a wild animal. A desperation that made her incredibly dangerous.

"Let Maggie go, Shannon."

Her eyes cut from the officers in the doorway to Reese. She drew herself up and yanked on Maggie's hair. Maggie winced and met his gaze. Terror mingled with fury.

"Tell them to get out!" Shannon screeched at him. "Out! Out! Or you'll never find Belle!"

Reese jerked his chin at Eli. The man shook his head. "Go," Reese said. "Shannon doesn't want to hurt anyone, do you? She just wants to be with Belle."

Shannon drew in a deep breath and some of the wildness left her eyes. "That's right. My Belle. Mine."

"Kent was going to take her away from you, wasn't he?"

Her lips tightened and she jerked a quick nod. Sorrow replaced the madness in her eyes. "He said I could have her. Then he said I couldn't." Confusion, then anger flashed. "But I got her anyway."

"You planned to kill him, didn't you? The night you hit him with the rental?"

"No." Shannon shook her head, the frown deepening the lines in her forehead. "No, I didn't plan it. It just… happened."

"Tell me how it happened," Reese coaxed, drawing on his negotiation skills. Skills he hadn't had to use in a long time. *Please, God, give me the words.* "Tell me."

She nodded to Eli and Cal who'd backed up, but hadn't left or lowered their weapons. "Tell them to leave."

Reese shot a glance at Eli then the window behind Shannon. Maggie's dark eyes stayed on him and he tried to convey his determination to make sure she got out of this alive.

Because Shannon had killed once. He had no doubts she would kill again.

NINETEEN

Maggie did her best not to struggle. Staying still was almost impossible with her head cocked at such a strange angle and her neck muscles protesting. But Shannon was talking to Reese. She was listening. And Maggie thought Shannon had lowered the gun a fraction. Shannon's grip on her hair wasn't quite so tight.

Eli and the others backed up. Eli met Reese's eyes briefly for a moment of silent communication that Maggie wished she understood. Then they were gone, leaving her alone with Reese and Shannon.

Shannon relaxed a bit, enabling Maggie to move her head slightly and ease her screaming neck muscles. Then Reese coaxed, "Tell me how it happened."

"My car was in the shop. I...I got a rental car that day and was going to a party that night." As she talked, she tensed again and Maggie winced as pain shot through her skull. Reese's eyes narrowed, but he didn't take them from Shannon.

"A party? Right, I saw that in the police report. You had an alibi for that night. They questioned you and the people at the party. You left the same time everyone else did."

From the corner of her eye, Maggie could see a sly grin cross the woman's lips. "I didn't plan it that way, it just…" Shannon shrugged. "It just worked out perfectly. Like God was telling me I was right and everything was going to be all right."

God? Maggie wanted to scream at the woman. *God doesn't condone murder.* She bit her lip and swallowed the words. So far Shannon hadn't killed her and Maggie didn't want to do anything to provoke her.

Reese said, "The police questioned you. Everyone said you were at the party all night and that you left when everyone else did."

"Of course. I felt ill and went to lie down. The hostess escorted me to a room on the second floor and told me to take as much time as I needed." Tension shook her. "The longer I lay there, the madder I got. I couldn't stand it. I called Kent and told him to meet me." Her words took on a singsong tone as she said, "He said he couldn't, he was busy. I knew what he was doing. He was gambling. Gambling away more money." A tremor shuddered through her. "He'd called earlier that day and told me I couldn't have the baby. I was shocked. I didn't understand. But I'm not stupid. I'm not stupid!"

"No one thinks you're stupid, Shannon." Reese's voice soothed, his body language conveyed confidence and an easygoing manner. But Maggie could see the coiled tension just below the surface. She didn't think Shannon would notice.

"Better not think I'm stupid. I'm not."

"You slipped out of the house, took the car and met him. And no one saw you leave?"

"No, apparently not. I didn't sneak out, but I didn't tell anyone I was leaving either. No one saw me slip out the back door, I guess."

"Or sneak back in," Reese said softly. "What happened? You met Kent…"

"And he told me that I couldn't have the baby. Just… flat out said I couldn't have her. He'd decided to keep her."

"Because of the money."

A growl erupted from Shannon's throat. "Yes, he'd found the envelope from Maggie's grandfather. And he said he had to keep Belle and kill Maggie and all his problems would be taken care of."

Maggie wanted to vomit. That someone could think so little of her life. Someone who'd professed to love her at one point. A wave of dizziness swept over her, and her neck cramped. And yet Shannon seemed to have forgotten about her. The woman was lost in her story, her memories, her hurt.

Maggie brought her hands to her chest and clasped them as though to pray. Reese's gaze flicked to her, then back to Shannon.

Shannon shifted, growing agitated. "But what about me? What about the fact that he'd promised me Belle? What about me! He didn't care about me! He laughed at me." Her voice dropped, chilling, the fury radiating as she remembered. "He laughed. Said I wasn't fit to be a mother anyway. And I just…lost it. I got in my car and while he was standing in the road laughing, I ran over him." She gave an eerie chuckle. "He stopped laughing."

The gun dipped and Maggie acted. She slammed her elbow back into Shannon's midsection.

Air whooshed from her lungs. The gun dropped to the floor and Maggie was finally free from the iron grip on her hair. She sank to the floor next to the gun and grabbed for it.

"No!" Shannon's screech cut off as Reese tackled her. Shannon's foot caught Maggie's hand and the gun skittered away from her.

Right next to Shannon's hand.

Shannon snagged it.

Reese's hand clamped down on her wrist, but still Shannon wasn't ready to give up. "Let me go! You can't do this to me! She's mine!"

Maggie's fist shot out, and she clipped the woman on the chin, stunning her. Shannon's eyes shot wide, and she went still as Reese stared at Maggie in shock—and pride.

Knuckles throbbing, Maggie silently thanked her police officer friend from church for her lessons in self-defense as she stared down at the woman who had caused her so much grief. "Belle and I were supposed to be kidnapped that day at the bank," she said, her voice low, terror for her own safety fading. "And then they were supposed to kill me, right?"

Shannon nodded, her eyes narrowing. "And then Belle would be found by the police and she would be given to me."

"Because my will stated that you would get Belle and the money that came with her. When that failed, you simply wanted that man, Douglas Patterson, to kill me. He shot at my house, Shannon. He could have killed all of us, including Belle!"

Shannon snorted. "That never should have happened. He was incompetent and stupid." Her eyes changed, glazed over as she said, "But it doesn't matter now. I have Belle. I'll always have Belle. She's mine." Then Shannon laughed. And laughed.

Maggie wanted to slug her again. "Where's my baby!"

But Shannon was beyond talking as Reese called for Eli to come in and take her away. The words *Psych ward* reached her ears as a violent tremor shuddered through her. Where was Belle?

* * *

Maggie felt as if she was going to fall apart. Reese rushed to her and wrapped his arms around her. "We're going to find her."

"She's okay. She's not hurt. Shannon may be mentally ill, but she wouldn't hurt Belle."

Eli stepped back inside. "Cal's here. He got Jason to the hospital and he's in surgery. Looks like he's going to make it. He's going with Shannon to the hospital to see if he can get any more information about Belle from her." He looked at Maggie. "We'll find her."

"Please," she whispered. The thought of never seeing her child again was more than she could bear. Tears flowed down her cheeks, and she allowed herself to lean against Reese, allowed him to comfort her for a brief moment.

Then she sniffed, stiffened and pulled away from him. "What can I do?"

"What?"

"I need to be doing something to find her. What can I do?"

He stared down at her and for a moment she thought he would tell her to let them handle it. But she couldn't. She needed to do something.

Eli said, "You can think. Think back on every conversation you had with Shannon. Did she ever tell you anything, say anything that would indicate that she was planning something? Where she could leave Belle while she dealt with you?"

Eli's phone rang and he answered it while Maggie forced her brain to cooperate. "I don't…" She shook her head. "I don't know. She talked a lot about missing Belle. She quit her job…"

"She was fired. We already looked into that."

"Oh."

Eli looked up from his phone. "And she bought four one-way tickets to Paris."

Maggie flinched. "Four?"

Simultaneously, Maggie and Reese said, "Her parents."

Eli hung up, dialed and barked orders. He looked at Maggie and Reese. "Let's head for the airport. Their flight leaves in forty-five minutes. Shannon may have told them to go on if she didn't make it."

"It's at least and hour and fifteen minutes to the airport. Can you stop the plane?" Maggie asked as she rushed out the door toward the police car.

"I'm working on it," Eli grunted as he slipped into the backseat. "Drive, Reese, while I try to stop that plane and give descriptions to security."

Reese drove. Maggie prayed and Eli consulted with airport security. She watched the clock. For the next forty-five minutes, she prayed and listened.

Eli finally said, "They're holding the plane."

"Have they found Belle?"

"Asheville P.D. is there looking for her. I had them pull up driver's license photos so they know what the Bennetts look like."

"It's not a very big airport. Why haven't they found them yet?" She bit her lip and closed her eyes on the panic threatening to swamp her.

"They could be in disguise."

"No, no, no. Please, God," she whispered. Reese reached over and grasped her hand with his. She drew comfort from his warmth, but felt his tension. She shuddered. "What if they see people looking for them? What if they get suspicious? What if—"

His hand tightened. "No what-if's. We're going to get her back."

Maggie clamped down on the fear and her panicky words. "Right. Of course we are. We have to."

Within minutes, Reese pulled up to the curb, lights flashing on top of the car. He held up his badge to security and the man waved them on.

Eli was back on the phone. "Where? Got it." He looked at Maggie and Reese. "This way."

They hurried through the crowd. Thanksgiving was in two days, she realized. People packed the airport. Rushing to the gate, they were met by TSA security officials who cleared them within minutes then escorted them to the gate. Airport security had been briefed and was anxious to help.

Maggie drew up short.

Sitting twenty yards away were Mr. and Mrs. Bennett. In Mrs. Bennett's lap was Belle. Security sat on either side of them.

Maggie rushed forward and dropped to her knees in front of her daughter. Belle squealed when she saw her and launched herself at her mother. Maggie caught her and rocked backward landing on her rear end, but holding Belle as close as she could without squeezing too hard. She breathed in her little girl scent, set her on the floor in front of her and ran her hands over every inch of her child.

She looked up at her former in-laws. "Why?"

"We didn't realize we were kidnapping her," Mr. Bennett said. "Security found us and told us what was going on. Shannon called and said she might not make the plane and for us to just go ahead and she'd catch up later. She said she had custody, that you signed her over. She showed us the will and spun a story that—" He broke off and a lone tear slid down his cheek. "We're sorry. I think we knew something was wrong, that there was no way you'd just sign her over, but we hoped…we wanted to believe so much…we're sorry."

She could see their grief, their pain. It all looked real, as if they truly had no idea what Shannon was doing. Maggie drew in a deep breath and felt some of her anger and bitterness toward this couple start to fall away. She stood and picked up Belle. To Reese, she said, "Will you check out their story? Make sure it's true?"

She nodded and looked at the grief-stricken husband and wife. "If what you say proves to be true, then I won't keep Belle from you. You can see her whenever you want."

Twin expressions of shock greeted her announcement. Mrs. Bennett blinked. "What?"

"Shannon was a con artist—and mentally ill. I can see how she could play on your grief for Kent and your desire to see Belle. I can't hold that against you." She paused and studied them. "If what you say is true."

"It's true," Mr. Bennett whispered. "I promise, it's true."

Mrs. Bennett gave a small cry and leaped to her feet. Throwing her arms around Maggie's neck, she whispered, "Thank you."

Maggie felt hope sweep through her. And relief. It was over. Her eyes met Reese's and the tender expression there made her gulp.

TWENTY

Maggie stood beside Belle's crib and simply watched the baby sleep. It had been three months since Shannon had tried to kill her and kidnap Belle, and Maggie still didn't like to take her eyes off her daughter.

But the fear and anxiety were fading. Reese had been a big part of helping her accept that the danger was over and she and Belle were safe.

All three bank robbers were serving time. Shannon was in a hospital for the criminally mentally ill and getting help. Maggie hadn't been able to bring herself to go see the woman yet, but she hoped one day she could do it. Reese assured her he thought she could.

Reese.

Love filled her heart.

"Hey." Warm hands settled on her shoulders and she turned to see the man she'd been thinking about.

"Hey."

"I got your groceries put away. I'm going in to work in about an hour. Are we still on for dinner?"

Maggie wrapped her arms around his waist. "I love you, Reese."

He froze, then a small sigh slipped from his lips. "I've been wanting to hear those words for a while now."

She looked up into his eyes. "I've been wanting to say them for a while now."

"So why now?"

She smiled. "Because it was time."

He looked at the sleeping baby then pulled her into the den. The fire crackled in the fireplace and through the window she could see a light layer of snow covering the ground.

Excitement flooded her. She'd finally said the words and now that she had, she was surprised at how easy it had been. And how much she wanted to say them again.

"I love you, too, Maggie."

The air in the room suddenly seemed too thin. "You don't have to say it just because—"

His finger covered her lips, cutting her off. "I've been wanting to say it since we found Belle at the airport." He reached into his pocket and pulled out a small box.

Maggie drew in a much-needed breath. She whispered, "Reese?"

"You and Belle have wriggled your way into my heart and…" He shrugged. "I have something I've been wanting to ask you, but didn't want to rush you."

Her stomach flipped. "What's that?"

He dropped to one knee. "Well, I was going to be a little more creative about this, but since you've provided the opening, I'm going to go ahead and step through."

"Reese?" She couldn't seem to say anything else. She felt shaky and light-headed and oh so happy. But first… "You're really okay with Belle, aren't you?"

He gave a sad smile. "I'll always miss Emma, but Belle is a beautiful little girl with her own personality, who makes me smile and has captured my heart. She's a part of you. How could I not love her?"

Maggie already knew that. She'd watched the two of

them bond like superglue over the past three months. They'd celebrate Belle's first birthday tomorrow and Reese had been like a kid in a candy store picking out the perfect present for her. "I know. I have no more doubts that you'll love her like your own." Eyes swimming with tears, she cupped his cheek. "You're already a father to her."

Reese's green eyes widened and he opened the box to pull out a beautiful diamond ring. "Will you marry me, Maggie?"

Her throat closed and all she could do was nod. "I would be honored."

He slid the ring on her finger and stood.

Belle's cry sounded and he placed a gentle kiss on her lips. "Hold on a minute, I'm not done."

Maggie sank onto the couch and studied the ring on her finger. Joy surged through her and she sent up a silent thank-you to God, who'd allowed Reese to come into her and Belle's life.

Reese walked back into the den with Belle on his hip. Belle lay her head on his shoulder and smiled at Maggie. Then Maggie noticed something on her daughter's tiny finger. A small silver ring.

She glanced at Reese. "One for her, too? How sweet."

He took it from her hand and said, "We'll keep it somewhere safe for when she's older. Right now, she'll just want to eat it." Maggie gave a watery laugh. He pulled her up from her seat on the couch and wrapped an arm around her shoulders. "This is my promise to be the kind of dad she needs. I promise to love her and teach her and train her in the ways God says fathers are to love, teach and train their children."

Her heart shook with emotion as he lifted her hand and kissed the ring he'd just placed there only moments before. "And I promise to be the kind of husband I'm supposed to be. I don't promise to be perfect, but I promise you'll never have reason to fear me."

She felt a tear slip down her cheek. "I can't believe I'm crying this much." He smiled and she said, "I love you."

"And I love you." He leaned over and placed another tender kiss on her willing lips.

Belle giggled and clapped and Maggie grinned through her tears. "Welcome home, Reese."

"Welcome home, Maggie." And she thought she heard him whisper, "Thank You, God, for my family." He planted a kiss on her forehead. "What's the first thing you want to do now that you don't have to worry about someone trying to kill you?"

Maggie thought about it then grinned. "Kiss you."

"I like that plan."

His head lowered but before his lips touched hers, she muttered, "Then put you in my will."

His laughter was music to her ears.

* * * * *

Dear Reader,

Thank you for joining Maggie and Reese on their suspenseful adventure to keep Maggie and Belle safe. Rose Mountain has become like home to me and I will miss it, as this is the last story in the series.

Maggie came from a broken home, but grew into a wonderful young woman who made a bad decision to marry a man who hid his violent side. Thankfully, she was delivered from that situation with the help of her grandfather and a friend.

Reese grew up in foster homes, but thanks to the love of one foster mother, he knew that he wanted to do something good with his life.

Our backgrounds and daily interactions with the people in our lives influence us greatly. I pray that you're the positive influence in someone's life. I pray that this story affects you in a way that makes you want to be a better person and trust the Lord a little more each day through good times and bad.

I love to hear from my readers, so if you want to visit my website at www.lynetteeason.com, you can sign up for my newsletter and keep updated with my latest writing news.

God Bless,

Lynette Eason

Questions for Discussion

1. Maggie had a rough few years with an abusive husband. What do you think of her decision to get out when she found out she was pregnant with Belle?

2. What do you think about her decision to go back to Kent before Belle was born? Do you think she was weak? Or strong?

3. Maggie is glad Kent is out of her life, but sad that he was dead. Are you surprised she would feel sad about that? How would you have felt if you had been in Maggie's shoes?

4. Maggie and Reese hit it off right away; however, he has a lot of pain in his past. He was raised by foster families and his heart's desire is to have a family of his own. He lost his and is afraid he'll never have one again. Then along comes Maggie and Belle. And yet he acts almost scared of Belle. Do you find his reaction odd? Or do you understand it? Why or why not?

5. Maggie is also an orphan in the sense that she has no more living relatives, other than Belle. What do you think about her decision to let Shannon back into her and Belle's lives? Do you think that isn't a very smart move? Or do you understand why she does it?

6. Maggie goes through a plethora of emotions during the time someone tries to kill her. She's scared, worried, angry and anxious. And rightly so. And yet she

turns to scripture during this time and trusts in God. What do you do when you're anxious or scared? Turn to God or away from Him?

7. What is your favorite scene in the book?

8. How does the story handle the theme of facing your fears and learning to trust again?

9. Discuss Shannon's motivations and her heart. How might the story have been different if Shannon had entrusted her life to God?

10. Reese finally gives in and lets Belle wrap him around her tiny finger. And it's only then that his heart starts to heal from his past wounds. What do you think about the scene where he volunteers to change her diaper and she ends up capturing his heart?

11. Maggie has a routine: she goes to the bank every Monday, she has Belle on a schedule and she has her teaching schedule. And she likes it that way. Are you a person who likes routine and schedules? Or are you more of an impulsive person who likes to toss such things out the window?

12. Maggie finally has to rely on others to help her stay safe. She'd relied on a police officer friend to help her get away from Kent—and then ended up not needing the officer's help when Kent was killed. And yet Maggie still uses some of those techniques to keep herself hidden, almost invisible, when she moves to Rose Mountain. Why do you think she needs to do that?

13. Reese is determined to get the person who's after Maggie. He couldn't help his wife and daughter, but this is something he *can* do. He can catch the bad guy for Maggie. What does this tell you about Reese's personality?

14. Maggie doesn't want to live off the money her grandfather left her. She lives simply and does her job every day while looking after Belle. What does this say about her personality?

15. Maggie gives Shannon a good punch at the end of the story. Does this surprise you? Why or why not?

REQUEST YOUR FREE BOOKS!
2 FREE RIVETING INSPIRATIONAL NOVELS
PLUS 2 FREE MYSTERY GIFTS

Love Inspired®
SUSPENSE

YES! Please send me 2 FREE Love Inspired® Suspense novels and my 2 FREE mystery gifts (gifts are worth about $10). After receiving them, if I don't wish to receive any more books, I can return the shipping statement marked "cancel". If I don't cancel, I will receive 4 brand-new novels every month and be billed just $4.49 per book in the U.S. or $4.99 per book in Canada. That's a saving of at least 22% off the cover price. It's quite a bargain! Shipping and handling is just 50¢ per book in the U.S. and 75¢ per book in Canada.* I understand that accepting the 2 free books and gifts places me under no obligation to buy anything. I can always return a shipment and cancel at any time. Even if I never buy another book, the two free books and gifts are mine to keep forever.

123/323 IDN FEHR

Name	(PLEASE PRINT)

Address	Apt. #

City	State/Prov.	Zip/Postal Code

Signature (if under 18, a parent or guardian must sign)

Mail to the **Reader Service:**
IN U.S.A.: P.O. Box 1867, Buffalo, NY 14240-1867
IN CANADA: P.O. Box 609, Fort Erie, Ontario L2A 5X3
Not valid for current subscribers to Love Inspired Suspense books.

**Are you a subscriber to Love Inspired Suspense
and want to receive the larger-print edition?
Call 1-800-873-8635 or visit www.ReaderService.com.**

* Terms and prices subject to change without notice. Prices do not include applicable taxes. Sales tax applicable in N.Y. Canadian residents will be charged applicable taxes. Offer not valid in Quebec. This offer is limited to one order per household. All orders subject to credit approval. Credit or debit balances in a customer's account(s) may be offset by any other outstanding balance owed by or to the customer. Please allow 4 to 6 weeks for delivery. Offer available while quantities last.

Your Privacy—The Reader Service is committed to protecting your privacy. Our Privacy Policy is available online at www.ReaderService.com or upon request from the Reader Service.

We make a portion of our mailing list available to reputable third parties that offer products we believe may interest you. If you prefer that we not exchange your name with third parties, or if you wish to clarify or modify your communication preferences, please visit us at www.ReaderService.com/consumerschoice or write to us at Reader Service Preference Service, P.O. Box 9062, Buffalo, NY 14269. Include your complete name and address.

LISUS11B

celebrating 15 YEARS

Love Inspired.

SUSPENSE

RIVETING INSPIRATIONAL ROMANCE

ASSIGNMENT: BLACKMAIL

Stephanie Gage's father has been kidnapped—by a dangerous man who wants to make a trade. Her beloved dad for a multimillion-dollar family heirloom that's gone missing. To track it down, she must rely on demolitions expert Tate Fuego— the man who broke her heart years ago. Stephanie knows that Tate's reasons for helping have nothing to do with her. But trusting Tate is all that stands between Stephanie and a madman's ultimate revenge.

Will Stephanie and Tate be able to find
the missing heirloom in time?

Find out in

DANGEROUS MELODY

by

DANA MENTINK

TREASURE SEEKERS

*Available
November 2012*

www.LoveInspiredBooks.com

LIS44513